Bill was a Theatre Manager at Epsom Playhouse as well as a Civil Servant for almost 39 years, serving the most vulnerable children and adults in the High Court. Taught English Literature by Peter Dale, the Modern Poet, he enjoys painting in oils and drawing in pastels.

For further updates, please visit: www.bill-webster-art.co.uk

D1369151

Dedication

For Bev, Eliot, Jana and Luka, Michelle and Monaie

Bill Webster

THE MAN OPPOSITE HAS DIED

Book One of the Sloping Meadow Trilogy

AUSTIN MACAULEY PUBLISHERS™

LONDON • CAMBRIDGE • NEW YORK • SHARJAH

A CIP catalogue record for this title is available from the British Library.

ISBN 9781787107137 (Paperback)
ISBN 9781787107144 (Hardback)
ISBN 9781787107151 (E-Book)

www.austinmacauley.com

First Published (2018)
Austin Macauley Publishers Ltd.
25 Canada Square
Canary Wharf
London
E14 5LQ

Acknowledgements

Mr Dale, Mr Holmwood and Mr Stoker who taught me English Literature at Glastonbury

Map of Area

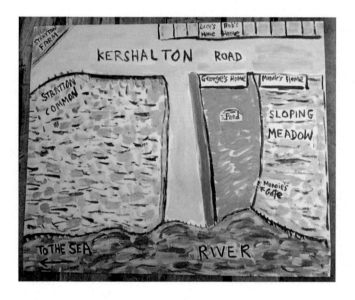

Chapter 1
Here Is the News

'The man opposite has died!'
The very first time I heard those words my inner voice told me "NO WAY!"

I am Lucy. I have long red hair and big blue eyes. I am an eight-year-old girl not used to anyone dying, never mind someone living opposite me, and then dying. Pete, my twelve-year-old brother, should have given us some sort of warning that we were about to be given a shock with his statement but he chose not to. Typical of Pete. He is a brother who is great company if you are on your own with him but put friends around you and he is a show off. Perhaps it was because the friends that I have surrounded myself with on this day in April are all younger than him and female. Who knows?

I lean towards him and say quietly in his ear "What?"

He pretends that he has not heard me, shifts from one leg to the other, clears his voice then says, like he was a newsreader, "George Davis has died this morning." He chooses to tell us in our front living room of our house which is directly opposite to where George Davis lives, or should I say lived. Let me tell you which friends I have with me and a bit about them so you can imagine the scene for yourself.

I have Claire with me. She is nine and pretty, or so everyone says. She has long dark hair to her middle back, is taller than my four foot, thin and always clean- looking even when the rest of us are not. She is my best friend at school and out of school. She can be a bit of a tomboy but can also dress very feminine when she goes out anywhere special. She is a bit of a mystery and I suppose that is what I like about her. I met her recently in McDonalds and she looked great in casual clothes.

Rob is the boy next door who is nine and always comes around almost every day after school just to hang out with us. He is blond haired and wears it long for a boy. I have always found him to be friendly and reliable: two very good traits for a friend. He is very careful about everything and I suppose a bit of a mummy's boy. For example, although he is strong he would never use his strength in a fight with any other boy in case his clothes become messed up in any way. He is a loyal friend and he loves whistling; any tune will do. Some of his female friends hate him whistling but personally I find it reassuring and think it could be so much worse. I find it amusing that we tend to hear his whistle before we actually see him. No matter how much food he eats he never seems to feel full up and as a result he is always hungry; often he will ask my mum, or anyone's mum for that matter, for food. He looks, for all the eating, very slim. He has green eyes and a friendly face.

Then I have with me Giselle who is ten. She has longish shoulder length brown hair and acts older than her age. I believe this may be because her parents are much older than our parents. Anyway, that's what mum says.

Giselle always tells us she has a mobile phone but none of us has seen it. I think this is definitely a lie. We call her Auntie for fun as she acts older than her age. Here is a photo of Giselle, Claire and I so you can see what we look like. Yes, that's me in the middle with Giselle looking all grown up at ten on your left and Claire on your right.

All friends dressing up. Except Giselle was "too old to dress up" (as if!) so only Claire and I did. That's the trouble with Giselle, she always acts older than her age. Giselle loves to please everyone but as mum says "it will just tire her out." We prefer her just being herself but there you are. We all get on most of the time and that, as mum says, is what matters.

Oh, by the way, here's a photo of my mum so you can see what she looks like. This was taken in March so it's recent. Mum thinks she can keep an eye on my older sister, Dora, by being on Facebook but she is, of course, well wrong. Don't let mum know this as she will be mad.

She is the coolest mum in the whole wide world and it's not just me who thinks so but all my friends. My mum is known as Katy and is twenty-eight but looks younger, or so dad keeps telling her. She was born Sheila but is known as Katy. Weird or what? Anyhow I think that most of the time I am blessed with a great mum and an okay dad. Dad spends most of his time either cleaning the car or under the car painting the inside of the wheels. Seems crazy to me but that's what dad likes doing. Once done he will spend hours, it seems, admiring the wheels like they are part of some new fashion show for car lovers that only he can see, oblivious to rain, sleet or even snow. I have no photos to hand of dad so don't expect one. Why should I have dad in my story?

To continue then Claire, Giselle and I are looking incredulously at my brother, Rob, having just been told that the man opposite has died. One of the first thoughts we all share was *well finally we can check out his pond and see if there really are newts in it!*

Giselle, eager to please as usual, then voices what we had all thought, "Let's go and pay George's garden a visit and see if there really are newts in his pond!" Immediately though, her older self comes to the front and she then adds, "We can't possibly do this as George, God bless him, has just died."

I speak with a smooth and soothing voice, "Look, if we are ever going to know whether there are newts in his pond this has to be the best time to find out – maybe not the happiest of times for George as he is no longer here with his wife, Vi, but he can hardly object now, can he?"

My friends nod to me in agreement. I smile trying not to look smug. Rob then finds it in himself to say rather proudly, "You will need someone strong to get over his garden gate. Don't think you'll get in unless someone climbs up and unfastens the bolt from the inside."

I say, "We could always ask a blond boy to assist us!"

Claire asks, "Who?"

I immediately respond with "Rob". Claire looks like she wants to hide her face away.

We all agree to do it after lunch but we will need a plan of action.

Suddenly Pete, more to Rob than anyone else, says, "I have seen old George putting varnish on that garden gate last week so it may ruin your clothes if you climb it, just saying…"

We decide in that moment in time that that my brother Pete will be climbing the garden gate but Rob will be giving him a hand up on account of his strength. End of. We agree to meet after lunch.

Chapter 2
Ridiq

George Davis is eighty-three but continues to work hard on his house and garden until he dies today. I have a photo which mum gave me to show you what he looks like (or what he looked like).

Mum says that he looks like Sir Michael Caine. I would not know as I do not know who Sir Michael Caine is. Mum says he was a good actor in his day. Anyway, here is a photo from mum to let you see what the poor man looked like before he died. Mum also says that George is rumoured to have a famous oil painting – a decent copy of a Degas painting. I don't even know who Degas was but mum says he was a great artist skilled in drawing people, horses and ballet dancers.

I have spoken to George when he was living, I think, twice in my lifetime. Once when we were allowed to carol-sing at his door and when we had sung our hearts out, he muttered, "Not bad for beginners," before giving us a pound coin. The second time was when my cat Billy went missing and he kindly unbolted, then opened his side gate, so my brother and I could look for him in their garden. On our way out he had observed that, "I hope you find your cat. Vi and I have no pets; the nearest we have to pets are the newts in the pond. They are like our pets although you can't see them now as it's winter. Come back in April and you can see them in the pond. You can also see the frogs – and hear them! But I prefer the newts."

A man after my own heart! I would have given anything in the world to have seen his newts.

All I can say about George with any certainty was that he seemed to have been a kind man – a kind, old man. And now a kind, old, dead man. Oh, before I forget, we did eventually find Billy in my chest of drawers, asleep under my best nightie, snoring.

George married Vi in 1957 and they had three children – all of whom live in Australia.

Look, before I forget, mum says I should let you see what Vi looks like. So here is a photo of Vi, his wife. No idea when this photo was taken but I think a couple of years ago.

Vi taught at the local primary school for years and George was a member of the church. Some sort of minister in the church mum says. They both retired together about eight years ago and lived quiet and happy lives until of course one of them had died. Mum says, in their own way, they were a lovely married couple. I am never going to marry – I think the whole idea sick – having a man telling me what to do for the rest of my days. Don't show this to mum. She would say "When you're older you'll understand." The only problem is that she says this to me in the same way as she says that I will like vegetables "when I'm older" so I tend not to take it all too seriously. I shall never marry. End of.

I have seen newts before, of course, but only in books at the library. I love all wildlife and creatures. Rob and I never forgot that day in December with the skies full of black billowy clouds and the smell of bonfires in the damp air and the promise of spotting the newts the following spring. What a great invitation! With George dead, this was unlikely to materialise. We must now surely find a way to make George's invitation remain intact so we can see the newts, if they really are there.

Oh, mum reminds me that George played the violin as she could hear the strains of a violin at night on weekdays when I was meant to be asleep (how can a girl possibly be expected to sleep when there are so many books that need attention?).

At first she thought it was Vi playing the instrument as she thought she 'looked more musical' than George but it was definitely George as once when he was playing, Vi appeared in the garden pruning the red roses.

Poor old George had died at the ripe old age of eighty-three. Who was going to play a sweet melody on his violin now? No-one. That was certain. Vi could hardly start now to learn the violin in time to play him off to Heaven. Mum says when you die you go immediately to Heaven. If I had my way I would abolish all death. I was so annoyed when I found out that someday we all had to die. Why should death come along and ruin everything? Why should death take our lives away? Mum informs me that "life is for the living" and in their own way parents can sometimes make some sense although their expressions such as, 'it's up to you' as mum says and, 'it's down to you' as dad says never make sense to me. How can the opposite words mean the same thing?

Rob and I play a game with our friends called RIDIQ which is short for 'ridiculous'. The game is easy to play. All you do is think up ridiculous statements and the most ridiculous one is the winner. If necessary, if in a group of friends, we vote for the best RIDIQ. Oh, you're better off not playing it if there are just two of you as you may just cancel each other out with your final choice. If there are more of you playing you can hopefully decide better by voting. Long live democracy.

Rob and I share the credit for this game as he had said something totally ridiculous one day and it was my idea to make it into a game. Try it yourself and see if you and your friends can come up with the most ridiculous statement. Just remember that Rob and I thought it up. How cool are we?

Chapter 3
Siamese Frogs

In the end it was my mum who fed us all at lunch and we then started to play RIDIQ in my living room before venturing out. Claire could think of very little in the way of ridiculous statements so she was content to sit and watch Rob, Giselle and I attempt to win as Pete, my brother, had exhausted all his ideas to win and had graciously given up.

"Just think up a statement that appears to **you** to be ridiculous," I whisper, helpfully, to Giselle on her final turn but I rather think she is far too sensible to be even associated with the ridiculous.

She then shocks me by squealing with delight "I am not here!"

We all laugh appreciatively.

"Well said, for you," we hear Rob enthuse.

Giselle is not best pleased and cries, "Just what do you mean by 'for me'?"

Rob lies. "I didn't mean anything by it! Just pleased that you are getting the hang of the game which I designed."

"Which **we** designed!" I shout.

"Okay. Which Lucy and I designed."

Rob then plays a blinder by declaring, "I don't know why I eat squirrels – they always make me cough." We all laugh at how ridiculous this statement is but into my head pops an even more ridiculous statement. Do I dare to annoy Rob and come out with it? Of course, I do.

"You have to be a nut to be liked by a squirrel!" I shout ecstatically to the sound of richly deserved laughter. Rob says, "Okay. I think Lucy wins today unless anyone else disagrees."

There is silence and I get to bask in my moment of glory.

Then in silence we all look at each other; hearts beating as one. We know the time has come for action.

Rob declares solemnly to us all, "Okay. I think we all know without going on too much that we need to be very secretive from now on. Tell no one what we are doing. Poor old George has died and we can finally get to see the newts in his pond, if they exist of course. First we have to cross the main road. Can I suggest that Claire and Lucy cross first and then hide behind the small fir tree and await the rest of us who will cross together?"

Pete then states, "Being the oldest here you have to be guided by me on most things. After all it is me who is going to risk my neck climbing over the gate. Do you all agree now that I have final say if we cannot agree on any matter?"

"We agree," I say for all of us. I was keen to press ahead to get to see the pond. No-one else said anything to contradict me. We all felt excitement ripple through our hearts and tummies. How cool is that feeling? Even better to share it with those you like.

Rob wore shorts and tee-shirt, as did Pete. Claire, Giselle and I all wore jeans and tee-shirts. We are now ready to face our adventure. The risk attached made it all the more worthwhile. Claire and I cross the road after waiting ages for the cars to clear out of our way and hide behind the small fir tree. The fir tree had its own strong smell of pines; this was not unpleasant. Shortly afterwards Pete comes over with Rob; both of them trying to look innocent and yet neither managing to quite pull it off. I could not swear to it but I'm sure Rob was whistling.

From our hiding place, we could see brave Pete square up to the imposing gate that belonged to the deceased George. Rob held out his joined hands for Pete to place his right foot into and within seconds Pete found himself on the very top of the tall gate once Rob had pushed him up high with the strength of a superhero.

"*WOW*!" we all thought. Moments later Pete had disappeared down the other side of the garden gate. After what appeared to be ages we all heard the sound of a large iron bolt being reluctantly forced back and, with a strong push from Rob from our side, the gate began opening.

"*WOW*!" we again all thought. The gate was then swiftly pushed to its most open by Rob with ease and we were inside shutting the gate as quickly as we could manage it. Our hearts were beating fast inside our chests as we realised we were in what appeared to be a garden that was full of the joys of spring! The sun shone like new crystal glass.

Blackbirds, trying to build their nests by scavenging twigs on the garden floor, scatter in disgust as we enter this paradise on Earth. I see a Robin perched on an apple tree branch which shows no fear of any of us. I understand at that precise moment why any man or woman would have wanted to live here; such was the great beauty of this garden in springtime.

Daffodils curtsey in the slight breeze to us in sheer delight. Just for say a minute we all are lost in the garden's beauty. All except Pete who has only just realised that he has been bleeding quite badly from a cut on his shin that he has obtained from his clambering down the other side of the gate. Claire manages to keep him calm by tying a ribbon taken from her hair around it. Luckily it soon brings success by helping to stem the bleeding shin. Pete winces in pain. He looks much older when he is in pain.

"Cheers," is all he says to her, relieved he is no longer in any danger. Claire simpers, "Oh, that's okay," suddenly embarrassed as she has only just realised that she has been, moments earlier, touching his bare leg with both her hands. For no real reason, she now feels shy and embarrassed about it. The feeling soon passes as she notices what we have all failed to notice.

A donkey is eating the long grass in the meadow next door to where we are. We all are pleasantly shocked. The donkey does not even look our way it is so engrossed in eating the lush, long grass which the meadow generously offers to it. Obligingly, the donkey eats to its heart content. The meadow is called Sloping Meadow. I am then aware of just how cool and moist the grass beneath our feet is in George's garden and, for that moment at least, the cool, moist air takes my breath away.

A young girl appears along the side of the donkey and, quick as a flash, we know that she is younger than us and also we know instinctively that she will not be any problem to us or our mission. She shows no fear and comes as close to us as she can in range of the fence but still managing to keep her balance among the bluebells. She looks slightly surreal standing there clutching a single bluebell. Pete leans over the fence and takes a photo of her. This is what she looks like. She told us her name is Monaie and her father owns Sloping Meadow as well as the donkey. She has evidently been allowed to look after it today while it was eating the long grass. We all like her and we believe she is about six. Isn't she cool? We wave goodbye to her across the fence and carry on.

Poor George's garden looks rich in colour. Many flowers are out, especially red pansies, purple pansies and white pansies and even I can recognise some species such as Michaelmas daisies and deep red and deep scarlet tulips that seem to have taken over most of one of the flower beds. They are resplendent and vibrant and all have happiness living inside them but somehow escaping slowly through their scent and through their beauty.

Just as we think we cannot remember where the pond is, Pete's mobile phone rings, startling all of us and making Claire jump.

"Hello, dad?" says Pete in a muffled voice.

"Peter, don't forget to remind mum I am playing golf till at least five p.m. today. Can't get her to pick up the house phone."

"Okay dad, will do," replies Pete.

We all then look at the expression on Pete's face. He looks surprised at seeing something. It then becomes clear. The pond is quite near – nearer than Pete and I had remembered when searching for the cat. It looks much smaller than before and greener now but this is because there has been so much growth of pond plants and pond weed since December. It is still a large pond. Large enough to house many living things.

"Lucy, you lead the way," mouths an excited Pete – the pupils of his eyes are large and I can tell, call it sisterly intuition, that he is happy to have made it here so far, almost unscathed. In his joy he completely forgets his aching leg. The pond has taken his mind off the pain.

"No," I say, "we can all walk slowly over to the pond and we can all do this together."

We all walk more or less together towards the pond. The nearer we are to the pond the shorter the grass appears to be, possibly because George and Vi loved to sit together, near the pond and wanted the grass to be short in the area where the nearest thing that they had to pets are here to be viewed – their newts.

It is the smell that hits me first. A strong smell of almost stagnant water but at the same time water that is full of life. We see water boatmen on the surface of the pond and all sorts of miniature creatures swimming about in the water itself. I manage to spot a dark green dragonfly high up, hovering like a tiny helicopter above the pond. Some of the creatures in the water look to me like small, shy prawns. Above the surface we spot mosquitoes annoying each other and lots of hoverflies showing off to each other. From the water's edge we search for many minutes for any signs of larger creatures and suddenly Rob shouts, "Look, Siamese frogs!"

I say, "What?"

Rob repeats, "Siamese frogs!"

Pete sees them clearly. They are two frogs – the smaller carrying the larger on his back. The frog at the back has its front arms clasped firmly around the neck of the one in front and looks like he is strangling her.

Pete instructs us, "These are not Siamese frogs – they are mating. That's how they mate and when she lays the frogspawn – he will fertilise it with his fluid. We did this in Biology. The frogspawn then will turn into tadpoles and the tadpoles will grow arms and legs and eventually, after losing their tails, they will evolve into baby frogs. Trust me." We did.

We are gobsmacked and stare at these two frogs that I had actually thought were fighting.

Mum always says that if you ever come across any unusual activity in life there is always some down to earth reason for it and not to be alarmed. Things happen for a reason; she tells me this often. She is usually right. Pete holds the pair of frogs in his hand high in the air so we can all view them but we persuade him rapidly to release them back into the pond to avoid any sort of harm coming to them. A huge *PLOP* later and the mating frogs are back in the water, using their instinct to swim down low into the depths of the pond and away from any danger. Pete thinks we are funny coming out with such things as 'Siamese frogs!' For the next few minutes I catch him chuckling to himself about Rob's remarks. Rob feels embarrassed for the next few minutes refusing to comment on anything. The word 'mating' really did not help much either but he soon forgets his embarrassment when he hears, then sees, a beautiful jay (my favourite bird) chase away a sparrow from its territory at the front of a pair of cedar trees.

I read somewhere that the jay, such a beautiful bird, actually belongs to the crow family. The only thing I can see the jay having in common with the crow is that they are both noisy birds.

Let me now try to describe the rest of the garden. Most of it is lawn but to one side of this lawn is an area where Vi and George have planted many fruit trees and they are now covered in white blossom; some of the blossom has fallen and is gently covering the land below; some of the fruit trees behind are evenly covered in pink blossom. I am not sure what type of fruit trees they are but I am sure of one thing – they look lovely. The blossoms that have fallen now remind me of snow. Both white snow and pink snow. I wish you could see this. It reminds me of Japanese paintings that I have seen in the library. At the back of the garden is a large, well built, wooden shed with what looks to me like a proper wooden roof on it. How cool is that? To the right side, facing the house is Sloping Meadow itself, now full of spring growth; even I can spot catkin and early thistles taking shape inside the rolling grasses of Sloping Meadow. Quite something. I can see buttercups and crocuses everywhere. How beautiful this garden is!

Never realised, until now, that you could have mauve crocuses.

How pretty these mauve crocuses are?

Chapter 4
Swept Off My Feet

"It's just like the Butterfly House at Whipsnade Zoo here," I say.

"Lucy, you are so right," whispers an excited Claire. "Only," she continues, "without the glass to keep them in."

"Yes," I agree, "And, what's more, I can see so many butterflies not only here but also in Sloping Meadow, where the donkey is."

No-one is at all surprised when out of the blue sky a Red Admiral lands on Pete's bad leg.

"Wow," Pete sighs. "It's like he knows I am hurting and... wants to make friends?"

"I would never have imagined that a garden could ever be as lovely as this one. Poor George will certainly miss it," is all that Giselle can say, in what appears to me, at least, as a very grown up tone. We all nod in agreement and sit down to feel the sun on our faces just for a short time. Rob forgets his earlier discomfort and says, "Would it not be just great to see some newts now?"

"Yes," I agree, "but **please** can we just go to the back windows of the house and see if we can spot George's oil painting, as mum says it's a copy of a real Degas painting?"

"I thought you were keen to see the newts!" cries Rob. "I mean, isn't that why we have come here, risking our necks?"

I say, "You're right, but I also need to be able to let mum know if the rumours that George had a copy of a famous oil painting in his house are true or not."

"Sure," Rob says, unconvincingly.

We all walk towards the house again accompanied this time by a braying donkey. The last thing we need right now is to be found on someone else's property. The noisy donkey could make other neighbours look at us from beyond Sloping Meadow or from the back gardens of the street.

"We should do what Lucy wants," says Giselle trying her level best not to be seen crossing the garden path.

At the window, I state the obvious, "I can't reach up to see."

It is Rob who answers my distress call by lifting me clean off my feet. (Now I know what it feels like to be swept off your feet by a boy!)

"Take as long as you need," Rob says confidently, holding me up perhaps higher than I need to be. *Thank God we brought Rob with us*, I think privately. I can feel his heart beating fast through both our tee-shirts and, if anything, it makes me even more nervous and excited. I can even smell the scent of the Fabric Conditioner his mum uses to wash his clothes. **Cherry Blossom & Sweet Pea**. I only know because mum uses it at times.

It really is not long before I am able to see into the lounge at what looks to me like a painting of two women in a place of work. Here is a photo taken just minutes later by Pete on his phone of what I had seen through the window. Can't wait to let mum know that the rumours are probably true. How cool is this oil painting?

On looking around poor George's lounge through the limitations of the glass window, still being held up by the superhero Rob, I then notice another oil painting which looks like someone has painted it straight onto the back of an oak door. I guess it must be about one metre high. It is of a Chinese lady. Rob thinks you should see this now so he asks Pete to take a photo of it. Hope you can see why I think it unusual. The more I find out about George the more I think I might have enjoyed his company, had he not died. Anyhow, here it is. Just how great is this?

Rob suddenly drops me hard to the grass floor.
THUD!
"Can't hold you anymore Lu. Sorry!"

"Oh," I respond, tying to remain cool, "that's fine. I have seen what I needed to and can now tell mum." Pete then walks right up to the window, positioning himself carefully like he was about to take a selfie, so he could then take more photos of the two artworks with his mobile phone then we once again crossed the garden path passing the two stone lions that guard George's back garden. The lions are made of quarried stone, hand-painted and both topped with manes that looked like real gold, reflecting the golden sunshine.They stand about four feet apart. We all feel happy. Happy to be here in this protected garden.

We are finally on our way to see if we can find and catch a newt or two just to say that we have actually done so. We are all excited. Rob is that excited that he forgets just for a while how hungry his tummy is feeling. He quietly whistles us along our way – all the way to the pond's edge. The light reflects majestically on the still water and the very top half of a silver birch can be seen as a reflection inside this shimmering light display. *We must be in Heaven* I think to myself.

After what appears to have been an age it is Claire who calls out to Rob, presumably for him to respond and catch it, "**NEWT**!"

Rob is too startled to do anything.

It is Pete who reacts like lightning. He catches what looks to me like a long thin fish that has just swam past the reeds.He stretches his whole body out on the grass bank as though this will prevent the newt from slipping back into the pond, now clutching the newt firmly to his chest. His tee-shirt is dappled with splashes of water from the struggle. It works. Soon we can see what we know now is a newt with a very long slippery looking tail. It has an orange belly with black spots.

Claire shrieks, "Well done, Pete, well done!"

Claire, in an effort to assist Pete, thinks she will try to help the situation by placing her thin body between Pete and the pond.

SPLASH! Claire falls straight into the pond and in moments she is taking it in turns to giggle hysterically then cry out in anguish as the cold pond water seeps first into her trainers and then through her jeans.The sight of Claire, who usually looks so clean and tidy with drenched trainers and soaking wet jeans up to her mid-thighs makes us all burst out in shrieks of laughter. Even the very bottom of her long dark hair is looking wet where she has tried to steady herself and has dipped it in the pond water. In the chaos Pete lets the newt slip back into the pond and it swims off towards a clump of pond weed.

Pete calls out, "She's escaped!"

Afterwards we tease him as to why he thinks the newt is female. He never did come up with a satisfactory answer; we never tire of teasing him about it. It took Claire some time to get over looking a bit of mess in front of us all but we love her for laughing so much at herself and for giving us such a laugh that day. The sun is not strong enough to dry Claire's clothing or trainers that afternoon in April but in all fairness to her she never once complains about the wet or the cold that she must have felt. Not to mention the fact that her clothes were no longer clean and smart.

For a long time to come we will remember, with the greatest of joy, just how happy we were in poor George's garden seeing the newt and knowing that George had been true to his word and that his pond definitely had newts in it. Just as he had told us once upon a time in December. Good old George! May he be blessed forever!

We do our level best to sight another newt that April afternoon but we fail to do so. Newts can be extremely elusive, it would appear. This did not detract in any way from the fun and laughter that we had shared; and all thanks to the lovely George. Now deceased.

At that very moment, Giselle, who was stretching herself out on the long grass to make herself better feel the sun on her face caressed the long, luxuriant grass with her hand and screamed out, not in joy but in horror. Her fingers had located a **FINGER** in the grass!

"**LUCY! THERE'S A FINGER IN THE GRASS!**" she declared in panic.

None of us could find our voices. All we could do was look in horror at an index finger, lying in the grass and stained with blood.

It is Pete who found his voice first

"Just do as I say. **Run – all of us – to the wooden shed over there**. Then we will discuss what to do next."

We do not need to be asked a second time. We run as fast as cheetahs chasing prey.

Chapter 5
A Place of Safety?

Rob arrives at the wooden shed first, closely followed by Pete, then Giselle, followed by Claire and me. We are breathless, with beating hearts from the effort. To say we are frightened is an understatement. We are terrified; we all find comfort and reassurance in Pete's next words:

"Let's try and get into this shed where we can at least plan our next move."

Claire tries the shed door knob but it is locked. She breaks into tears, and, out of breath, says finally, "Pete, it won't open."

"Don't start crying now – it's not going to help us – just hinder us."

I say, "Search for a key, sometimes people leave keys nearby."

Giselle starts looking in the long grass and at once we hear some movement behind us.

Our hearts all go straight into our mouths. If you have never experienced this, you will not believe me but I promise you our hearts are now IN OUR MOUTHS.

Rob whispers, "Relax, it's a hedgehog, you lot disturbed it," and, sure enough, we witness a small hedgehog scuttle sleepily towards the shed and disappear under it. The grass around the shed is dry so I am not surprised that the hedgehog made such a noise moving through it. Needless to say, we all breathe again a great sigh of relief. Claire, I can see is now frantically biting one of her nails and trying to stop herself shaking. I am also shaking but I am trying not to show it. I have never bitten my nails and I am proud of this fact. For the next few seconds we then all get mesmerised watching a large fat-bellied spider repair his web outside the shed's only glass window.

This is a photo of that same fat-bellied spider on the front of the glass, taken by Pete.

Claire finds the key on a ledge of wood at the side of the door and hands it over to Pete who gingerly opens the lock and the door opens. The smell of oil paints and petrol for the mower as well as books – old musty books – hits us with a force. I can also smell the very wood that the shed is built of. There is definitely more heat above our waists than below. We all feel that heat.

We shut the shed door rapidly with the minimum of sound. Pete instinctively sits on the carpeted floor and we join him, happy to be as far away for now as we can from that bloody finger.

Outside the window we can see the fat-bellied spider still working hard to repair its web. We can see the sunshine reflecting on the surface of the very web itself. We are now aware of Claire sobbing quietly to herself. After a few seconds, she wails, "So she **must** have killed George?"

"Who must have killed George?" snaps Rob.

"Why, his wife, Vi," replies Claire.

"What a primary school teacher?" Pete says in anger.

"Yeah, then she must have cut him up. Cut poor old George up and we have found his finger."

"No way," I say quietly. "Mum says it's very rare for a woman to kill her own husband."

"Your mum never said it was impossible though, did she?"

"I guess not," I respond, slightly disturbed by her words.

Pete adjusts his position on the shed floor to make himself more comfortable, moving his phone out of his jeans pocket onto a nearby shelf containing tools, small pots of glue and paint.

"I am unconvinced that Vi, a primary school teacher, married to a church minister, or whatever he was when alive, would want to kill him and then cut him up. It just doesn't fit. Anything could have happened."

"Look Pete, George is dead," I assert, "and she, as likely as not, is still alive. Now she may or may not have killed him but we need to watch her very closely from now on and when we are sure of anything we will tell the police and our parents."

Pete stands up and we all mirror his action. He is unhappy about a lot of things but I think right now he needs to show us calm leadership.

"Damn!" he says bashing his hand on a long piece of wood jutting out from a whole bundle of what appear to be logs. "A splinter!"

He sucks the side of his hand but is unable to retrieve the splinter even when he uses his teeth like pliers, so instead he just says out aloud,

"Look, I am not sure what has happened here but we need to all go home. We now need to do what Lucy has suggested and just watch this place and Vi. The moment we think we have evidence of anything bad happening to George we act and we tell the police and our parents. Can I suggest we all go home now? Slowly and very carefully!"

"What does evidence mean, Pete?" I enquire.

"It just means proof. When we have proof we can consider what to do next, okay?"

"Okay, Pete. Okay."

Silently, we all nod our heads in agreement.

Rob reminds us to replace the key taken from the ledge outside and we do this after locking the shed.

We make our way back up the path through the gate which we lock, with Rob this time doing the final climb over, after bolting the gate from the garden side. Before we cross the main road, Pete takes one final minute of our time to insist

"Do not discuss this with anyone! Until we know the facts we cannot really be sure of anything!"

Silently we show our agreement and head home. It is about five thirty p.m. and we arrive home hungry and much the worse for wear and feeling more grown up than ever now that we have experience of murder most foul.

Mum asks me what we have done and I say, "not much, mum." She smiles and kisses me noisily on the side of my hair like parents manage to do every time you perhaps don't always want them to. This kissing usually makes your ear goes deaf for a few seconds but the upside is you feel loved.

She smells of baking, more especially, of flapjacks. In fact, the whole kitchen area smells of flapjacks!

Can't wait to try one I think to myself.

And I do.

Chapter 6
We See a Ghost

I am fast asleep dreaming of newts, hedgehogs and Siamese frogs – the sort of things that most girls my age love to dream of – when I am rudely interrupted by a *Tap! Tap! Tap!* on my bedroom window. Sounds like someone is throwing stones at the window. On the brink of calling out for my dad I decide to investigate for myself.

Down at the back of my house, in our garden, in the darkness, but by the light of the moon I can just make out from my window Rob, then Pete, then Claire and finally Giselle looking up at me. None is smiling. Everyone, except Rob, has stones in the palms of their hands, which they now release to the ground.

Rob signals me impatiently to come down and to remind me to be quiet he holds one finger up to his lips.

Of all the signs to make, a finger, I think, but I have received the message and will obey once I am dressed in my outdoor clothes. I glide down the hallway and straight down the stairs without a sound and manage to reach and undo the bolt of the back door leading to my garden by quietly standing on a chair nearby.

"Pete's rather cleverly left his phone and we need to go back," Rob informs me.

"Go back where?" I reply half-asleep.

"To the shed. Pete thinks he must have left it there."

"Okay," I whisper. "Let me just put my trainers on."

I do and we go.

It is ten thirty p.m. and I should be back in bed, as should all of us, but we are not; we are going back to the garden where we think poor George met his death by murder most foul and where he lost his index finger, to retrieve Pete's phone, left in the shed we believe. We can all see why we have to go back but none of us wants to return there especially not at night, in the cold darkness.

We see foxes scampering around trying in vain to leap up and open the lids of the wheelie bins put out by neighbours but little else as we head off past the adjacent alleyway and to the main road. A small red car with a soft top speeds past us startling us with its big bright head lamps. The moon is out and affords us some light, enough anyway to see each other's anxious faces. Rob breaks the silence by whistling.

"Shush!" we all say together as soon as he starts and we laugh at how we all shushed him up at once. Even Rob laughs.

"I'm hungry," he declares as though we should have all known and we all respond with "Shut up Rob!" He laughs and enjoys us teasing him. Mum says people will only tease you if they like you.

At the gate, we manage to re-open it and close it again without injury this time and we are soon in the garden looking out for each other and feeling a slight chill in the night air. We cross the path, go past the cedar trees and make our way towards the shed but before we do we hear the strains of a violin. We stop in our tracks. We are frightened – of that have no doubt.

Someone is playing a violin in George's house. BUT IT CAN'T BE GEORGE.

"It could well be his spirit come back from the dead," Giselle says and we all feel goose bumps travel down our arms. We shiver.

I say "**Oh My God!**" Giselle repeats this and Rob's blond hair stands on end in fear! His green eyes look massive. His usually friendly face is now white with shock. He is most definitely not alone in his fear.

"I know," says Claire. "Let's just go straight home now while we still can!"

"We can't because Pete has left his phone and it is better all-round if no-one finds it before we do," Rob states matter-of-factly.

"Oh Bother! Bother!" sighs Claire, shivering again with the cold and with the fear.

Valiantly we continue towards the shed, find the key, open the door and shut ourselves inside within four seconds.

It is, however, so much darker than our earlier visit when we had watched the fat-bellied spider.

Pete finds his phone and uses the light on it to look for matches and a candle which he manages to find surprisingly quickly. Before we can praise him up for this great find he tells us dryly, "Oh, I spotted them earlier."

Rob offers to light the candle but Pete, as the oldest, feels responsible for all of us and lights it easily. This action throws eerie shadows on the shed walls and ceiling. I now realise that if we had not been in such a state with what is going on with George we could have perhaps enjoyed this evening a lot. For all the danger around us tonight we feel relatively safe and warm inside the late George's shed.

I can appreciate that having a shed when you retire can be a great and wonderful thing and is not to be knocked when you see just how many things George has packed into it. It has become his secret cave. Everything is here that is needed to perform all the tasks of managing the best garden in the street, including the lawnmower, still with a whiff of petrol around it. I feel worried about everything but do, nonetheless, feel safe with Rob and Pete here with us. We all now hear the ghostly strains of George's violin again.

From the shed we now see a shape move inside the house and it is possibly female. We decide to leave our place of safety and investigate. We need to see what is going on.

"All stay together," Claire reminds us all.

We do not, however, need to be reminded. We all walk as one out of the shed leaving the candle burning. In any other circumstances, we would have looked like we were in a comedy film. At least, by leaving the candle alight, we can see to make our way back there if need be.

Almost bending down, we creep slowly towards the house to minimise our shapes and sizes.

We notice not just one light on in the house but quite a few. As we approach one of the lights, we spot what looks like Vi's shape walk across a main room. We expect her to be here – probably packing up for the last time and readying herself to leave – perhaps tonight, perhaps tomorrow. Who knows? Who really knows what a murderer is about to do next? When she leaves, we will have a good look around the house if we can get in. She cannot be allowed to see us though. Of that we are sure. Where has she hidden the rest of George?

She looks like she is packing bags; perhaps she will leave the house tonight and we can have a look around when she leaves. Perhaps she will leave tomorrow on the train after packing up all the money she can get her greedy hands on. One by one most of the lights of the house darken and only one light upstairs now remains on.

Just then Rob breaks the silence of the night with, "Can you guys smell burning wood?"

"Eh, no, Rob we can't," Claire says convincingly.

I say, "I can. Why?"

Rob responds with "I think maybe the shed is on fire. LOOK! We have to put it out."

In the moonlight, we all then notice dark smoke coming from the shed area behind us, floating lazily up in the light April breeze.

"Yup, we must go back and put the fire out," Pete says, "The candle must have burned down to the wick and the flame has spread to the shelf. We have to try to use the water in the pond to extinguish any flames. Look out for any containers or buckets, anything that we can use to fill up with water and put out the fire. Hurry!"

Giselle trips up in her haste to reach the shed area first. Fortunately, she has tripped up on a plastic garden bowl that we can possibly use to gather water for the fire.

"There is no time to lose!" screams Claire. "I can now see yellow flames and they are getting larger and longer!"

I say, more to my brother Pete, than to anyone else, "We must try to put out the flames but safely put them out. We cannot panic now. Mum says never panic as it can encourage others to panic."

Pete puts his arm around me and says, "I wish mum was here now but she is not. We have to do what we can

47

in the circumstances. I cannot endanger your life, my little sister."

I blush with the emotion of what he has said and swallow hard thanking my lucky stars that he is here with me. I do love my brother but I would never tell him.

Claire and Rob are so near to the fire in the shed that they shout, "The fire has made the whole shed area hot. We cannot go into the shed now. It is too late."

The shed is now ablaze with the fire and the heat is becoming more intense.

Pete, remembering the petrol for the mower is in there, shouts out loud: "Rob, Claire and Giselle come away now or the whole shed could explode and kill us all. There's petrol in there!"

In the blaze, all of us look into the shed window one last time, catching our own reflections and then we are blown away by seeing George's ghost standing there in the smoke of the fire, looking at us coldly from inside the shed.

GEORGE'S GHOST is inside the shed!

I am only eight but it was all too much for me. With the speed of a comet crossing the sky I run with Rob gripping my arm and the arm of Giselle. Claire runs, gripping the arm of Pete. We are disorientated and we are heading straight for Sloping Meadow where we saw the donkey earlier. We need to be heading the other way. We are doing what mum has told me not to do – panic. We are in a state of panic. We all think it, and then we all say out loud, very loud: **"OH MY GOD!"**

The smoke is thicker now and we can hear the sound of cans of paint exploding inside the burning shed and we are desperate to avoid any sort of major explosion from the petrol held in the shed for the lawnmower. With superhuman effort, we carry on running as far as we can from the shed.

We all fall down what I think at first to be a badger's sett but I later realise is a large hole where George kept all the compost. This is green stuff that turns into mulch and is spread on the garden to help the flowers or vegetables grow. To say it smelt bad is an understatement. It stank. It was gross.

Pete put his phone light on and we soon realise that we are a long way from the house which now has the moon behind it making it appear even more unfriendly and even more ghostly.

At that moment, we hear a very loud wailing sound and see the flashing lights of a fire engine between the cedar trees.

"**OH MY GOD!**" I scream out and both Rob and Pete repeat it. Then amidst all the noise we hear a small shrill voice calling through the night air.

"Over here! Over here!" At first I think it is Claire who has maybe fallen somewhere and needs help but with the aid of Pete's phone light I can now see we are near the meadow fence and right next to the fence is the little girl called Monaie.

"If you carry on down you will find a wooden gate that I have already opened for you to escape into my dad's meadow. I heard noises and saw the black smoke from my bedroom window next door then I saw the mobile phone's light and thought it must be you lot. I can show you how to walk out of Sloping Meadow in the dark but you must go through the gate first."

"Yes, it is us… and thanks… we do need your help, desperately. You see we cannot be found on this property just at this moment in time," explains Rob, "and what's more I can't possibly tell you why we cannot be found, either."

Rob then runs knowing that we have no choice but to follow him as fast and as furiously as we are able to in the dark.

Monaie has saved our necks and we are grateful. She then went back to her bed as we did promptly. What a lovely young friend Monaie had turned out to be. How cool is she?

Chapter 7
Back to Sloping Meadow

The night before, on parting, we have arranged to meet up with Monaie, more to say thanks to her for helping us escape from the situation we had found ourselves in the night before, than anything else.

Pete is the only one to spot a police car pulling up outside George's home but says nothing to anyone.

It is ten a.m. and, as agreed, we meet directly outside Monaie's house. The smiling Monaie appears.

Pete, being the oldest among us, presents her with a token of our appreciation, wrapped up in kitchen roll.

"What is it?" she asks.

We all reply together, "Open it and see!"

Monaie unwraps it and is delighted.

"A kite shaped like a real butterfly. How sweet. Thank you so much." Although only six, Monaie has been well brought up and now feels embarrassed with us all looking at her various expressions of six-year-old joy. She dances with natural joy, almost skipping.

She leads us down her pathways at the back of her house and into Sloping Meadow where the donkey is once again eating the long, luscious grass. Today is hotter than yesterday. Mum has already consulted her iPhone and told me, "It will be twenty-seven degrees with a fifteen percent chance of heavy rain."

Mum has also already told me this morning about the fire last night and it was hard for me to pretend I knew nothing. But pretend I did.

Claire is the first to speak once we are in Sloping Meadow.

"Monaie. It was so brave of you to come out last night and help us to come through your gate into this meadow to escape the fire and the fire brigade."

"Yes," she replies, "I thought I was brave as well."

We all laugh because of what she says but she does not understand why we are laughing, so, very quickly Giselle says to her, "You have a great dress on today."

"Thank you so much," she responds and a smile as big as a teacup crosses her face. She is a lovely looking child and smiling, and her were made for each other. She is very articulate for her age and has dark brown eyes that come to life when she is interested or excited in conversations.

I was walking in front of Rob and Pete but now I am in line with Claire, Giselle and little Monaie. We walk for a long time before we come across a river at the side of the meadow. I would guess it is about three metres wide and it is Rob who spots a wooden boat with oars inside on the river.

"Shall we take the boat across?" he squeaks with excitement.

"Eh, Monaie, have you ever been to the other side of the river?" Pete almost demands of her.

"Dad has but I have not," she replies quickly.

"Look, we are all good swimmers but are you, Monaie?"

"Dad taught me to swim. I am a good swimmer now."

Soon we are in the boat and Giselle and Claire are paddling us along the river towards the other side. In the hot sun, we are happy and we are all pleased to have sun cream on as we may have burned our skins. Our parents are very good at sun cream. When you get the taste of it in your mouth though, it is horrible.

From the boat, we can view stickleback fish and in the deeper parts we thought we spotted larger fish but did not know their names. Pete pulls his water bottle from his rucksack and asks: "Anyone ready for a drink?"

We all have drinks except for Monaie. She tells us that she is "okay".

We see an otter swim across to the riverside that we have just left and we feel it is going to be a good day.

In no time at all we land the little boat on the other bank of the river and all get out.

Just as we have all embarked a large and snarling dog appears about thirty yards away.

"That looks like an American Pit Bull. Get back in the boat all of you! Now!"

With that Pete grabs little Monaie and more or less throws her into the boat but not hard enough to hurt her. Pete then comes for me clutching me and pushing me hard into the boat. Claire clambers back in the boat and grabs a paddle to defend us. Pete is now in the boat clutching the other paddle and we think we are safe but Giselle suddenly screams out.

"Help! The dog has cornered me!" she declares.

I look over from my upside-down position in the boat to see Giselle and then see that the dog has her pinned against two trees that are growing intertwined on the river bank. This ferocious beast is now barking and, more worryingly, snarling at her. It is getting too near her now.

"Keep calm," cries out Rob and, mustering all his courage, climbs out the boat and charges at the dog with a paddle stolen from Pete. The dog jumps at Rob and literally pushes him straight over and down into the boat again as though he was nothing. The boat begins to move out from the bank with the force from the dog. We hear an almighty *SPLASH!* Followed by another almighty *SPLASH!*

The first splash is Giselle swimming frantically for the boat. The second splash is the dog swimming frantically for the boat.

As the dog reaches the boat Giselle make it to the safety of the back of the boat then climbs in. Rob has no choice now and crashes the paddle onto the dog's head. The dog will not give up however and, although it yelps in pain, it continues to swim after the boat across the width of the river. It is now three yards away from the boat, barking and howling like it is possessed by a demon. White saliva shows on the dog's lips.

Suddenly the dog stops. It stops swimming and whimpers. It is not looking at us anymore but has seen something behind us and stares at it. The dog immediately turns back and swims for its own bank.

We turn around.

A lone figure is on the other river bank. It is the ghost of George staring at us and then slowly moving away from us towards his old home on the other side of the meadow.

SAVED BY THE GHOST OF GEORGE.

We turn back to face the dog but it has also disappeared.

At that moment, it starts to rain and I realise that mum was right again – a fifteen percent chance of heavy rain.

The rain increases in strength and might; we are now getting drenched. Little Monaie is now completely saturated by the water and her dress is sticking to her body, making her look like a dishevelled doll. Her dark hair is flat against her head. She is still smiling though.

We are all soaked to our very skins.

"Thank God that our skins are waterproof," Claire shouts above the sound of the rain bucketing down now. And we begin to laugh and never stop laughing until we climb out of the boat on our side of the river bank to where we saw George's ghost.

Pete coolly observes with scientific accuracy

"NO FOOTPRINTS. THIS CONFIRMS THAT IT WAS A GHOST. HE WAS STANDING RIGHT HERE!"

We stop laughing.

How uncool is that?

Chapter 8
Tea with Monaie

We head back now with heavy hearts. Only Monaie is still smiling. She is pleased to be with us and invites us in to a red bricked country house full of charm

"Please have Tea with dad and I. Dad will have lit the wood burner by now and you can get warmer and drier."

"How thoughtful you are Monaie. How can any of us resist?" Rob replies for all of us.

As we nod in agreement, rain runs down our faces and onto the wet grass making us all laugh again. We now follow Monaie into her large house which is full of the scent of wood burning. Rob says, "How lovely! The smell of logs burning in the wood burner."

"It is great to be out of the rain and inside the warmth of the house," I say.

Monaie's dad says, "Looks like we have company," and opens the lounge door revealing a wood burner full of logs burning brightly in the fireplace. For a short time, the light thrown out by the fire hurts our eyes. It is that bright.

"Thought I would get rid of the chill in the air," he continues, looking at his fire with pride. "You lot look very wet indeed so you better get nearer the heat."

He then asks Monaie to introduce us to him and Monaie confuses Pete for Rob and vice-versa. We laugh and keep laughing, especially when she pronounces Giselle as "Gyselle". Monaie continues to smile politely and treats us all to cake and tea, which her dad pours out for each one of us.

Without meaning to, Monaie suddenly blurts out.

"Dad, we saw a ghost!"

Our hearts miss a beat. We are too shocked to respond. Outside the fine rain is, I believe, turning to coarse rain. We again feel safe in this friendly home.

Monaie's dad is a large man with large chunky knuckles and a tattoo of an anchor on his forearm. He has a permanently ruddy face – some say on account of being fond of red wine – some say on account of being outside in the elements all day. Who knows? Possibly a mixture of the two would be my guess. He has sweet, kind eyes, the colour of autumn grass. He smokes a small hand carved pipe and can make smoke rings. We are fascinated by this. He spends most of his time in the Sloping Meadow training horses for events. He does this on a very long lead. It is not his favourite thing to do because he prefers flying light aircraft which he sadly cannot afford to do now since his expensive divorce from Monaie's mum, a lady well known in the village of Kershalton. Like most men he does not always listen to everything said to him by females but, after what appears to be some while, he puts one more kiln dried log on the wood burner and smiles as it slowly begins to char, then smoke and then burn.

In his mind, he is reliving a memory from long ago on a ship in the sea, just off the coast of Gibraltar. His smile now goes away.

57

"Saw a ghost once when I was about twenty."

He keeps us all waiting for so long to continue that I shout impatiently, "What happened?"

He smiles another ruddy smile at me then turns his large head towards Rob, Giselle, Claire and Pete. He declares quietly,

"We should not have even been out that day, the weather was so bad!"

He has now captured our full attention.

I laugh nervously and Monaie snuggles up to me.

Out of the windows of their lounge I can see the weather is closing in and heavy rain has made the sky turn the colour of burnt toast. If I strain my eyes I can still see in the far distance their donkey soaked to its fur but still eating the wet grasses. From this height, I can see why the meadow is called Sloping Meadow; it slopes aesthetically down towards the river. I can see how majestic this meadow really is. I can see why I am pleased to be here in the dry and in the warm, looking out at Sloping Meadow full of heavy weather.

The smell of the new log burning – actually an ash log – is intoxicating not only to me but to all of us sitting there desperately trying to feel warmer after our experiences at the other side of Sloping Meadow. It really does belong to Monaie's dad. Passed down to him by a great aunt who ran out of relatives to leave it to in her will. In turn, no doubt, Monaie will be left Sloping Meadow to enjoy for the rest of her days. I hope so, if only so we can still see it and her.

Her dad resumes his tale. He now looks like a weather-beaten pirate telling a story from his past. The fire is now reflecting in his eyes, making everything he says, seem like a tale from another world.

"It was seven a.m. when we left the Port of Gibraltar. We had no idea just how strong the wind could get around there but we soon found out. It was almost three hours later, whilst heading for the Spanish coast, that we nearly lost the ship. The weather was impossibly bad. We took water aboard the ship and we were on the brink of taking too much water on when we saw her."

"Saw who?" I cry out, unable to wait for him to tell me.

Monaie tells me, "Dad will tell you if you just wait." We all laugh and again Monaie is unsure of why we are laughing but delighted that we have reacted to her words.

Her dad, oblivious to the sounds of our laughter, now begins to sing some sort of sea shanty learned, no doubt, when he was a sailor on a ship:

"Blow them down when the waves get stronger,
Blow them down when the sea breeze comes,
And let them see that we are stronger.
Stronger than the waves ahead."

We all grip our arms and feel intoxicated by the tale.

"We see the mermaid," he says, "and she was pointing to the east away from the rocks."

"Was she real?" cries out Giselle.

"Not real. Not one bit real. She kept coming and going."

"What do you mean by coming and going?" Rob asks frantically.

"Disappearing then reappearing!" replies Monaie's dad. "It was she who saved the ship and all the crew that day."

Then he goes quiet and he never speaks again that night. The sound of the logs burning we can hear but we are no longer going to be hearing the sound of Monaie's dad's voice not until we see him again.

He sits down next to Pete, wipes his brow of sweat that has materialised on his forehead and looks exhausted. He certainly has relived his ordeal in the sea at twenty.

Whether it was the heat from the fire or the thoughts we were all now having we all felt tired, very tired and were happy to just try and soak up the atmosphere in this lovely old home that belonged to Monaie.

I, for one, can recall the sound of the logs banging as the fire heated them up.

Bang! Bang! Bang!

BANG! BANG! BANG!

Chapter 9
The Brain Is an Amazing Thing

The logs continue to make their banging sounds in the fire. *BANG! BANG! BANG!* I am now aware of someone banging at the door. Loudly banging.

BANG! BANG! BANG!

And again, *BANG! BANG! BANG!*

I rush to the door amazed that no-one else bothers to answer the door.

"It's mum," a voice says rapidly.

It is my mum's voice that I hear now.

"There's been a massive flash flood, Lucy. Our home and this home are now at risk of movement."

Just as my mum finishes speaking I can hear the sound of running water. I rush to the window and now see, unbelievably, that we are surrounded, whichever direction I care to look in, with water. Dirty brown water. Deep water because it is now up to just below the windows. We are in trouble for sure.

My mum shouts now, "If we can stay in the house we may be alright."

Mum could not be more wrong because without any warning at all the house begins to move slowly at first and then begins to gather speed.

It is now rapidly moving down Sloping Meadow. We are moving like in some fantastic action film. Only we are the unfortunates, caught up in what appears to be a sudden and terrible landslide of terror.

Rob and Pete stare out, mesmerised by fear at the torrential flood. Their eyes have widened with the sheer scale and horror of it all. Between them they cannot find a way of stopping this onslaught of Mother Nature. They both are powerless to help me or Monaie or Giselle or Claire or Monaie's dad or my mum, for that matter.

Did Monaie's dad bring this on us with the talk of ghosts and sailing ships? I privately wonder.

"How did it suddenly get so bad?" Rob asks anyone who can hear him.

"We have no idea," we all say in response.

My mum seems so calm that I then think that perhaps all can still be well. Who knows?

"Climb up!" my mum shouts above the noise of the catastrophe.

She then shouts louder: "**Climb up! Climb up!**"

But then she changes and seems to be now saying **"WAKE UP! WAKE UP!"**

Why would she be saying that?

"Wake up Lucy, wake up, you fell asleep and are dreaming."

It's Claire's voice now and not my mum's.

"Oh my God!" I say and Rob, Pete, Monaie, Giselle and Claire all repeat together "Oh My God!"

"The brain is an amazing thing," I murmur and we all laugh together. I cannot tell you how relieved I am that it is just a dream.

Outside it is raining but not nearly as bad as in my dream. It must have been the heat from the wood burner that sent me to sleep.

We can now hear the sound of snoring and we laugh again as we can hear Monaie's dad, lost in deep sleep, snoring loudly. It sounds like he is choking at times.

Rob, Pete, Claire, Giselle and I then thank Monaie for a lovely time.

I do not thank anyone for my dream.

We head out of their lovely home and make our way back to our houses. We have had quite a long, hard day and need now to get back so we can eat and decide what to do next.

Pete now arranges for us all to meet at six p.m. tonight outside his house so we can discuss where we go from here. Who knows?

Chapter 10
The Best Laid Plans

I can hear Rob before I see him as he is whistling loudly this time.

"Hi Rob," I say. "You are definitely the first to arrive."

Soon the others arrive. Not Monaie, as she is having her bath.

Pete announces to us all, "I have decided. We need to go back to George's garden again but this time through Monaie's gate so we need permission from her dad to go into Sloping Meadow."

"Why, Pete?" I enquire.

"Because we have a need to ascertain if Vi has left the house for good or, indeed, what she is doing."

"You mean we are going to be like spies," Claire says.

"Yes, if you like," replies Pete.

We knock on the old oak door that belongs to Monaie's dad.

After ages Monaie's dad answers the door.

"Hello youngsters, what would you like? Oh, by the way, didn't mean to scare any of you earlier with my old tales from the sea."

"Oh, that's fine," I lie. It was not fine because he still scares me even now as I look at him.

He gives me a lovely, ruddy smile and a pirate's wink, and I forgive him instantly.

Taking advantage of his good mood I say, "Can we please go back and play in Sloping Meadow tonight, just to see the donkey and admire the meadow flowers?"

"Any friends of Monaie's are mine," he responds.

Before he can say another word we quickly walk past him through his lovely open French windows and out into the back garden where we pick up the main path for the majestic Sloping Meadow.

Rob leads the way and we follow closely behind him.

After a few minutes, we leave behind the orderly flowerbeds and short grass of their immediate back garden and now come through the meandering path that will take us into the meadowlands.

On the paths, I notice the sticky trails left by snails earlier in the wet weather.

We can see an open area as a likely spot where we think that Monaie's dad trains the horses that are brought here and we can see evidence that they have been here; we can see their old hoof prints all over the flattened and patchy grass, as well as their droppings. The smell of the horses lingers a long time in this well-worn area.

Finally, we follow Rob into Sloping Meadow; all of us taking in the air and the view simultaneously.

We are glad to be back but we all notice that dusk is not far away as the light is less than it was a few minutes ago. Darkness will creep up on us like a ghost.

"If we can just get through this gate we will be into George's garden," Rob states, engrossed in trying to remember where the shed was in relation to where we are now.

"No wonder," he continues, "I was looking for a shed still standing. No wonder I can't see it now."

We eventually come across the old burnt out wreck of George's shed each one of us sharing guilt over the shed's fate. Someone has been here because some of the items that we had earlier seen inside the confines of the shed are now outside it.

"The least we say about the shed the better," I say and I think we all quickly reach agreement on that.

"Let's just say we could have done better on the shed situation," Giselle says and we all smile a guilty smile at her wit. Giselle has reacted well to what has been happening to her.

"Let's crack on and see if we can get up near the house now. Remember it is still better that no-one spots us up here so keep low and hidden as much as you are able to."

We all agree with Pete and make our way through the wet grasses of the meadow enjoying the sound of singing birds.

I murmur, "Perhaps they are thrushes."

"Yeah maybe sis, maybe," Pete replies, and gives me a big brotherly hug.

"Just a second," Rob says sharply, "look over there."

We do and it is clear even from where we are standing that two men, perhaps around twenty-four or twenty-five, are retrieving something from Monaie's dad's land.

Giselle exclaims: "Why, it looks like they are taking money out of a tin box in the ground and placing it in a plastic bag."

The two men look and act suspicious.

"Try to get nearer without them spotting you."

"I will, Rob," says Pete, "but I think I need to go around those trees to cover my movements, or they will see me."

"Go on then Pete, we will wait here hidden by these bushes," he responds, pointing to some bushes about two metres from us.

"Stay quiet and I will try," says Pete and then disappears from our view to chase a path towards the trees.

We are all worried now for Pete as these men look desperate and dangerous.

The men take it in turns to look furtively around them and we stare out hidden by the bushes now.

We can now see Pete crossing around trees and slowly reaching to where they are.

"Stupid kids in the area!" One of the men says angrily as Pete, for all his earlier success at hiding from view, suddenly finds he is now in full view of them and only about twelve metres away.

The men gather what is left of the money from the ground and place it into the bag and run away from Pete's direction but towards our direction.

We do not panic but wait, trusting the bushes that we have befriended, to protect us. They do.

The men run past, leaving a strong smell of cigarettes in the air, leaving us panting with the sheer effort of trying not to make a sound. After some minutes Pete joins us, with an apology.

"Sorry about that, everyone, guess I'm just not that used to being a spy."

Giselle says, "Pete, you did very well, better than I could have done."

"Never mind. Can I suggest that we follow them, just to see where they go?" Claire says.

"I know where they are going," I say triumphantly.

"Where?" Four voices ask me at once.

"Towards Monaie's house."

"So we have to follow as bravely as we can," I state and no-one disagrees.

We all run together and this time we need to run fast towards trouble to help Monaie in the event she needs our help.

We reach the end of Sloping Meadow exhausted but realise the two men have now barged right through the side hedge near the house to get out into the farm lanes. We carry on to the house running through the French Windows and through the open front door to be met by a blue horse truck revving up and ready to go. It looks fifty years old but is strong.

We are certainly surprised to say the least.

"Oh my God!" I say and I then look inside the truck to be surprised again by Monaie's dad sitting there in the driver's seat with Monaie on his lap, smiling.

"Get in all of you. We saw the men approach the back of the house. Let's follow them in the truck and see why they were on my land."

We all climb in and sit on the long seat next to Monaie's dad. We explain what we saw. There is plenty of room and we are all excited and scared to death all rolled into one. With difficulty, we leave the drive and end up chugging along the road hoping that we will spot the two men but also hoping that we are not hurt by them. We have Monaie's dad with us and we have each other for support. We outnumber them.

The blue horse truck has seen better days, as they say, but does its level best to get us moving along after much white smoke has appeared out of its exhaust.

A few bangs later from its tired engine and we are now on our way in hot pursuit of the two men.

Monaie's dad is quite a character and although he does not have a radio in the blue horse truck he tells us, "I can sing to you all if you like." We graciously decline but none-the less he has succeeded in making us laugh.

Rob, Pete and I are nearer the path side window than the others and we cry out.

"The two men there, crossing Farm Lane. Can you see them?"

The others say a resounding, "Yeah!"

Monaie's dad tries to slow down a bit but we skid a while then hit a car, an old Mercedes car, full of bits and pieces. It happens to be their car. They jump into this even more battered than it was before car and head off down the road with us in pursuit. We have given no thought to what they may do to us but we have Monaie's dad and Pete and Rob and you know somehow we feel what we are doing is justified.

"Had the money come from some legitimate source," Pete explains, "they would not be running away."

Monaie's dad says, "I agree."

I say, "What does legitimate mean?"

Pete says, "It just means honestly obtained by them. Look, the money is definitely dodgy, if you see what I mean."

"Think so, Pete," I respond.

And I think to myself. *HOW COOL IS THAT?*

Chapter 11
We Consult a Fortune Teller

After a few more miles, we all realise that we are in the dual carriageway that leads up to Stratton's Farm – the largest farm around here – covering roughly a hundred acres of rich agricultural land. In fact, before the turn of the century, it used to be known as One Hundred Acre Farm.

In days gone by, Stratton Village was a well-known market, to buy horses and many came from far and wide until it became a very popular horse-trading market. From then on it became even more popular than Kershalton Village that specialised only in lavender. The Strattons were very pleased with its success.

When the Strattons moved in they did two things, mum told me. They changed the name of the farm and also the name of the common land (that the public have always had a right to walk through) to Stratton Common. Local people called them scum and believe that they had paid with dodgy money to get what they wanted, especially with the change of name of the public land, now known as Stratton Common.

The Mercedes went left, then right and we followed it closely but after a police car on duty had more or less forced our blue horse truck to come to a halt whilst it negotiated the up and coming crossroads we could no longer see the Mercedes.

"We did what we could," says Claire.

"Looks like we have lost the Merc," agrees Giselle.

On Stratton Common Road we then see the fair. This is the annual fair that takes place in the second week of spring. The lights and sounds of the loud music and the fairground rides resonate in our ears now as we drive slowly past. We can feel through the truck the fair's throbbing vibrations, caused by the loud music and the loud engines running the fairground rides and the rides themselves.

There are dodgem cars, a wide coconut shy and a large wheel with folks screaming in their thin seats as they sway in the wind.

We see a rifle range and more bright lights, and then Monaie finally pleads with her dad,

"Can't we just get out and stretch our legs?"

Translated this means 'please, can we enjoy the fair like everyone else seems to be?'

Monaie's dad, possibly tired with the driving, announces, much to our joy, "Looks like we are going to the fair!"

We park the blue horse truck and only on getting out do we realise just how uncomfortable it has been to travel in. Our legs feel heavy and a bit achy. We are very pleased, however, to be out at night and at the fair.

Rob asks Monaie's dad if we can have a go on the dodgems and Monaie's dad agrees.

He insists though that Pete phones his parents and lets them know where we are and that we could be late. Pete asks them, thoughtfully, to let Claire's and Giselle's and Rob's parents know. He does this as quickly as he can.

We all race to where the bright multi-coloured and multi-flashing lights of the dodgem cars are and, in no time at all, we are crashing and bumping the cars into each other. Rob is in a car with Pete and they crash into a car holding Monaie and her dad. Giselle, in a car on her own, shocks us by just what a great dodgem car driver she is, steering away from crashes constantly. I told you she is a mystery. Claire and I are hit so many times that we begin to feel sick and are pleased when the horn sounds for the end of the ride.

Then we head off and Monaie's dad enjoys showing off his great shooting skills on the rifle range winning Monaie a huge pink teddy.

On the way back to the truck, we then spot a small tent with the sign:

GET YOUR FORTUNE TOLD.

It's Pete's idea to ask Monaie's dad if we can pay and have our fortune read. He makes out a convincing argument by saying:

"If they really are fortune tellers, they should know where the two men went and should be able to tell us."

It is amazing how someone's idea when given in the right place and at the right time can take off and become accepted by all. This one was definitely one of those great ideas. We all felt that the two men had got off scot free and needed to be taught a lesson.

It was agreed that we would first ask if we could all go in together and the lady who was the fortune teller took our money then we all crowded in to what really was a very small tent with a small table on which was placed a crystal ball – this is, for those of you who are unsure, a glass ball in which the lady was going to stare, slightly above it to try to read our fortune. We agreed that Rob should be the chosen one to have his fortune read. The lady allowed Pete to take her photo. It is so you can see what she looks like. To us she looked very proud and very mysterious indeed.

The skin on her lips was dry and peeling and she spoke in a whisper, adding to her mystery.

"The crystal ball clearly shows me a donkey and a blue horse truck."

"WOW," we all exclaim.

"Can you see anywhere where the Mercedes might be now – we were following a Mercedes and lost it?" Rob helpfully tells her.

"I can now see the words clearly in the mists of the crystal ball"

She then says the words she sees **"Stratton Farm."**

We are gobsmacked and barely take the time to thank her before running out towards the blue horse truck. Monaie's dad treats us all to hotdogs before we speed away. Soon we are all settled in our seats and Monaie's dad is driving us noisily and erratically towards Stratton Farm. The smell of the hotdogs is in the air and in the car, and now is on our clothes.

Night is now closing in. On the road, the blue horse truck's lights show the cat's eyes embedded in the middle of the country lanes leading us to the outskirts of Stratton Farm.

Will the fortune teller prove correct? Will we find the Merc?

Chapter 12
Stratton Farm

With the best will in the world it is now going to be difficult to find an excuse for calling on the Strattons at eight fifteen p.m.

Rob, however, comes up with one, "Tell them you have come to pick up a donkey from the farm and have brought your kids along for the ride."

"Well done!" I say and even Monaie thinks it might work but her dad is worried.

He responds with "Okay. But just stay in the truck you lot!"

We agree and so when the truck pulls up to a large sign stating **STRATTON FARM** we are quiet and wait our further orders. We park the blue horse truck.

Monaie's dad knocks hard and confidently at the large imposing door of the farmhouse and we peer out in the darkness for any signs of life.

"What are you doing? This is private property and you are trespassing!" says a rough, loud male voice through the door.

"Hello matey," Monaie's dad shouts in his best pirate voice. "Come to collect the donkey for the Production of 'Joseph and the Amazing Technicolor Dreamcoat'!"

The door opens and a little rogue of a man with grey wisps of hair on an otherwise bald head replies, "You what mate?"

"Come to collect the donkey for the show in London!"

"No you haven't," says the little man.

"Are you calling me a liar?" Monaie's dad says, trying to sound hurt.

"Not a liar but you aren't picking up any critter here cos we don't have any critters here… except James," the man then laughs, loud and long.

James, it now appears, is another man living there as he comes out and says to him, "You calling me a critter?"

"If the cap fits, wear it!"

At that James punches him hard on his arm and James then addresses Monaie's dad. "Look matey, don't know where you want to go but it is not here."

"You don't have any fields here with donkeys in awaiting collection. Are you sure?"

"Of course I'm sure. I'll get a torch and show you."

James gets a torch and takes Monaie's dad outside the porch area and around the back where he shines the powerful torch on the area behind, the beam of the torch hitting what looks like an old Mercedes car.

"Alright matey," Monaie's dad concedes. "You don't look like you got any donkeys here at all. Sorry to have troubled you. No Sat Nav you see. Got lost."

"And no sense either," the other man says, just loud enough to be heard.

Monaie's dad, in the circumstances, chooses to ignore it and responds, "Alright matey, best get on our ways then. Sorry to have troubled you."

The two men close their door behind them after watching Monaie's dad get into the truck and drive away.

We travel down the road and the truck is brought to a sudden halt whereupon I say,

"So, the fortune teller was wrong then."

"No she was not, little one; quite the opposite. She was absolutely right. Saw the old Mercedes car right in their back yard. The idiot shone his torch on it."

We are surprised and excited now.

Pete says, "What now then?"

Monaie's dad replies "We park here and go to the back of the farm and see what we can see."

"What, all of us?" Monaie says.

Her dad replies, "Unless you don't want to come".

"Of course I WANT TO," she cries out loudly.

I am feeling a bit tired now but decide that we are so near to finding out what the men were doing in Sloping Meadow that I have to stay with it all.

We head off now having left the safety of the blue horse truck and aim for the back of Stratton Farm and towards who know what.

Darkness takes hold of the night now covering it with a blanket of mist. The moon cannot be seen as the mists obscure it. Only the faintest scent of fruit tree blossom can be detected by me. Normally, this would bring joy to my senses but I also have a sense of menace coming to me now, and I shiver.

Chapter 13
Tight Rope

Making our way briskly along a country lane at the side of Stratton Farm we soon come across a lane that takes us around the back of the farm and, risking everything, we climb over a lower fence and are now at the rear of the farm.

Pete occasionally uses the light from his phone but cannot do this for long periods or we will be spotted and we do not know where the two men are. We can all feel the chill in the air and are wary that we do not know our way around here. We are not familiar with the ways of the men who operate here. We are not familiar with their rules of fair play.

We notice what is a very large cowshed, or what used to be a very large cowshed. We peer into the dirty window and see our two men counting money.

"I suppose," says Pete, "they have to keep themselves occupied."

"They'll hear you," I say with sisterly regard.

"Huh? Oh, sorry sis," he now whispers.

Monaie's dad is all for returning to the blue horse truck and phoning the police, asking them to check out the situation here and reporting what we had seen the men doing at Sloping Meadow.

Rob disagrees and offers, "Why don't we try to lock them in first?"

"We do not have access to the key," replies Monaie's dad.

"If you look closely you can see the key hanging up near the inside of the door." I have said what I think.

"My thoughts precisely, Lucy," replies Rob. "We sneak in or rather one of us does and..."

"**AND WHAT?**" says a very loud voice.

We are caught, all of us, and they are carrying what look like to me like long curved swords, although it is dark and I could be wrong.

"Oh My God!" I say.

"God won't help you now so no point in involving him," says the shorter man.

The taller one shouts out to the shorter one, "Get them in the cowshed and tie them all up tight!"

"Do as they ask," Monaie's dad tells us quietly.

We do. We are not ready to do battle with long curved swords.

Soon all of us are tied very tightly. We are then left in the middle of the large cowshed building on the cold concrete floor.

It is only Rob who has the presence of mind in the turmoil to take the key on his way in to the large cowshed building from the wall near the inside door and place it inside his hands.

It is also only him who uses a very old trick and makes his hands and arms as wide and as big as possible creating the impression that he is being tightly bound up with rope when, in fact, he is not.

The tall man then says to the two men, "Get rid of the Mercedes, or we will be swamped by the police. Take it out far away into the countryside and set fire to it. The money and all the bags will be flown out of here tonight. Before you go you need to load up the plane. Now hurry!"

"Yes Boss," they both reply to the tall Stratton.

Monaie's dad looks directly at Pete and Rob before winking, as much to imply, if only these two Strattons remain here and are all we have to deal with, then we may have a chance of getting out of here. Rob manages to begin the long task of undoing his ropes which have not been tied as tightly as ours have been.

The two men now begin the lengthy job of moving all the money in white bags and all the other stuff in white bags into the plane. Because of the time they take to walk back from the plane we all calculate that the plane has to be just outside the large cowshed where we are being kept against our will.

Rob manages to keep on untying his ropes without anyone noticing him.

It has been a great effort on his part. I can see that his cheeks are bright red with the efforts he has been making.

They tied Monaie up next to her dad and she has now thankfully fallen asleep.

The tall Stratton now agrees that the two men may now leave in the Mercedes and they go.

The shorter Stratton now informs his brother,

"I will now get the plane ready for take-off and put the runway lights on."

The taller Stratton says, "We need to get out of this country and never return. We will have more than enough money to stay in France for the rest of our days."

They both now have to help each other to get the money bags and the other bags into the plane because there are so many to carry.

Rob now uses this opportunity to escape from the large cowshed building to outside, running towards the front of the farm.

I have to make a very large distraction so we can all get away he thinks.

And he does.

He goes into the farmhouse, finds some matches and sets fire to the curtains of the lounge.

This will set off any fire alarms, get them in here to put the fire out...the last thing they want is the police around here before they can escape... and hopefully give us time to escape. This is what he thinks.

It begins to work. The two Strattons hear the fire alarms going off and charge into the blazing farmhouse.

Rob runs to the large cowshed building and begins to set free Pete, then Monaie's dad, and they in turn manage to free everyone else.

"Quick!" the Strattons say to each other, "Get back to the cowshed and check on them all!"

This is exactly what we are waiting on and as soon as they enter the cowshed and start looking around for us, Rob locks the pair of them inside.

Meanwhile Monaie's dad has easily started the plane.

The green lights of the runway are on and we are on the way towards the runway in a moving plane.

Rob is congratulated by all of us for his brilliant strategy.

He really has done so well in making sound decisions that have saved us today.

From inside the plane, Monaie's dad instructs Pete to phone the police and tell them there has been a fire at Stratton Farm and that we have a small light plane full of money and bags of stolen items that we will be landing at Sloping Meadow soon, if all goes to plan. And can they have fire crews standing by on Sloping Meadow, just in case of any difficulties in landing.

Monaie wakes up and for the second time in her life she is in a plane being piloted by her dad.

We put all our trust in him to get us safely home to Sloping Meadow.

The plane's action is bumpy now to say the least but using all his flying skills Monaie's dad gets the little plane to take off and then circle the area of Stratton Farm. We all hear the wheels used for take-off now going back inside the undercarriage of the small plane.

Below we can see small clouds of black smoke coming up from the large farm. Hopefully, the police and fire crews will reach the cowshed before it is too late for the two Stratton brothers.

We are airborne now and enjoying it.

We all enjoy flying, especially when I tell them all that mum says it is the safest form of travel.

Perhaps I have spoken too soon.

It really is not long before the plane is right above Sloping Meadow and ready for landing.

"I'm just putting the wheels down now for landing on, so you may hear something," Monaie's dad says to us all calmly.

We then hear nothing. No wheels are coming down.

Monaie's dad now says, "We now have to circle for about ten minutes while I jettison some fuel. I can't get the landing wheels to come down."

I say, "What does jettison mean?"

Monaie's dad replies, "Get rid of."

We jettison lots of fuel. We do this right over the sewage farm at Bedlington, and Monaie's dad tells us the fuel should just evaporate eventually so will not cause harm to anything.

Now we are heading towards Sloping Meadow again with very little fuel and no landing wheels.

"OH MY DEAR GOD," all of us, except for Monaie's dad, say out aloud.

Monaie's dad is totally focussed on what he knows will be a difficult landing.

He is calm.

I am terrified but I have to trust in the skills of our pilot.

The plane turns one last time away from our planned landing site – Sloping Meadow – and then majestically ascends to enable it to descend again in line with the contours of Sloping Meadow.

We have fallen below clouds and now we can make out the many shades of green in the late George's garden and can see the shape of the donkey, now the details of the donkey. We can clearly see the dear friend we call Sloping Meadow. The beauty of Sloping Meadow is being magnified by the second as we descend.

Monaie's dad declares in his calm voice, "We have no landing wheels so this will be rough. Everyone lean forward in your seats and expect a lot of noise."

Monaie is thankfully still asleep.

Our ears begin to pop as we crouch down with our hands covering our heads. Under my tee-shirt, I can feel my heart beating rapidly, and my tongue feels very dry.

Chapter 14
Mother Nature Protects

There is a noise now like thunder as we descend further and start to hit the ground.

The noise is Monaie's dad putting the plane, after touch down, almost immediately into reverse thrust to help the plane slow down so we do not catch fire. There is a risk that, since we have no wheels, the friction caused by the plane's body and the ground rubbing at great speed could easily set off a fire.

This is exactly what happens.

Sliding along at an incredible speed we become suddenly aware that just under both of the plane's wings we can see fire spreading. Every so often there is a *THWACK* as we hit a bush and cut it to pieces with the plane's undercarriage.

We must be doing seventy miles an hour now as we speed along the foliage of Sloping Meadow not knowing when we may be stopping.

The fire is, if anything, getting worse but intermittently the flames disappear then suddenly will reappear to our horror.

"We have to come to a standstill soon," Pete reassures me.

I respond with, "Sure hope so, Pete, for all our sakes."

Rob and Claire are next to each and look like they are praying; certainly, both their hands are shaped like praying hands.

Giselle is rather cool looking and is completely absorbed in watching Monaie's dad steering for all his worth what is left of our plane.

Finally, Monaie's dad shouts, above the noise of destruction going on all around us,

"At least the Strattons' plane is well built. It is doing what it should be doing – keeping us alive."

The plane is still intermittently on fire. We can now feel the heat from these worrying fires. There is a smell of engine oil and aviation fuel in the plane itself.

Giselle has stopped staring at Monaie's dad and now says

"We are definitely slowing down now."

I think *how cool is Giselle?*

The plane is being controlled as best as the pilot can control it.

We are still on fire as we start to slow down.

A huge cheer goes up inside the plane as we all come to realise that we are in fact now heading slowly for the river, which you will remember is at the bottom of Sloping Meadow.

I would guess our speed to be about thirty miles an hour.

If only we can actually reach the river we will be safe from the fire as the water will presumably put the fire out. This is our hope. If this can happen anywhere it has to be in the place we love, Sloping Meadow.

The plane now makes more noise than ever as Monaie's dad applies full brakes to the plane but we have no wheels so we keep on sliding down towards the river.

Our speed is now about three miles per hour.

The river extinguishes the flames with great hissing sounds and this deafens us as we begin to scrape first along the concrete bunkers at the edge of the river then topple slightly straight into the river.

The plane floats!

THE PLANE ACTUALLY FLOATS ON THE WATER.

WE ARE STILL ALIVE AND WELL.

We all cheer and applaud the pilot.

And then, after all we have been through, we start to sink in the deep water.

WE NOW START TO SINK!

"At least we have no fire now," Rob shouts loudly.

"One by one jump out through the plane doors and swim to the first bit of bank that you can find," Monaie's dad directs.

He grabs the sleeping Monaie and we all do as we are instructed.

Rob and Pete rather gallantly await us alighting into the cold river before they jump in oblivious to the cold water and pleased to be alive.

Thankfully, we can all swim and have no further difficulties in getting to the bank side with the aid of Pete's phone light and the lights from the plane.

Incredibly the plane remains afloat for a further five full minutes and then with great gurgling sounds and a rushing sound of water it sinks low into the water. Only the very top of it remains on view now and we all give thanks to Monaie's dad for saving our lives.

"Piece of cake," he says with a wink but we know that he is definitely joking so we laugh loud and long.

We then hear the wail of police cars coming across Sloping Meadow towards us and we are glad at least that we are safe and no longer have to deal with those awful Stratton brothers.

Chapter 15
Arrested Development

The first police Range Rover pulls up next to us, driven by a burly PC, and a WPC steps out.

She carefully avoids the ground up mud from the plane landing earlier in the evening.

The night is dark still but we benefit from the lights of the Range Rovers and their flashing blue lights, all making it easier to see.

She is in ordinary clothes so she must be important. On her lapel is a badge that tells us that she is Chief Inspector Layton. We are sitting on the river bank completely wet, exhausted and now cold when she struts up to us and delivers a remarkable and unexpected speech: "Frank Darby, I am arresting you on suspicion of theft of a Light Aircraft and false imprisonment of children. You have the right to remain silent. If you do say anything what you say can be used against you in a court of law. You have the right to consult with a lawyer and have a lawyer present during questioning. If you cannot afford a lawyer one will be appointed for you if you so desire."

Monaie's dad exercises his right to remain silent. He is quickly handcuffed and placed into the Range Rover. I notice blood on one of his cheeks.

We are quickly covered in thin metallic sheets to keep us warm. I have seen these sheets before at the London Marathon.

Pete quickly takes a photo of the chief inspector so you can now see what she looks like. Although she realises the photo has been taken she chooses to take no action, possibly because Pete is a minor. Two uniformed

WPCs step out of the second police Land Rover and take all the children into their Land Rover. We are no longer afraid of anything after all that we have endured. We are just very, very tired. We get in and remain silent.

The only sounds in the night are those of the police radios that crackle away before we can hear voices that are possibly miles away –or even nearer perhaps and possibly at Stratton Farm. Who knows? I remain calm because at times like this I recall my mum's wise words, 'if you are in trouble it never does any good to make a fuss, not at least until you have carefully thought about just what you wish to make a fuss about.'

It was now about eleven thirty p.m. Our parents knew we were with Monaie's dad but that was all. It is true that we are now in Sloping Meadow, where they would have thought we might have been, so that is still true to this moment. If they had known that we had been to a fair and been in a plane, and involved with the notorious Strattons, they just would find it hard to believe.

If, however, they had been told that Monaie's dad, who was responsible for our well-being and care, has now been arrested for stealing a plane and for taking children hostage well that would be almost impossible.

We are taken to Kershalton Police Office.

Soon we are surrounded by many social workers who overwhelm us with their questions and with their insinuations that perhaps Monaie's dad has been out to harm us in some way.

We defend him emphatically.

"No," we say, "Monaie's dad did not force us to do anything that we did not want to. Monaie's dad was our hero and saved all our lives."

Monaie is so tired now that she merely lies on the floor and sleeps soundly, only occasionally asking for her dad. Her dad is not there but being interrogated rigorously by two police officers.

After much time and, with us all feeling exhausted, we are collected by our parents and taken to our respective homes. Monaie's dad is bailed and will have to return for more questioning in the future.

Monaie is finally allowed to be taken home to Sloping Meadows with her dad.

Everything is not well with our parents but, I believe, on advice from the police and the social workers, we are not to be heavily questioned, thankfully, and will be allowed to sleep.

We accept this offer with relief.

We fall rapidly asleep. We do not stir until well after nine p.m. the following day.

There is more to all of this than we can imagine but the next day we learn from Monaie's dad that all is not well. For him this matter will not be dropped; not by the police nor by the Strattons.

Chapter 16
Arson As Well

I learn on waking that my parents are not best pleased with Monaie's dad for apparently risking our lives in the plane.

They will not discuss anything that happened and have chosen to only talk about it all when I am not there so I go out and meet the others. My parents blame Monaie's dad for everything. I think this unfair but I have no great say as Lucy the eight-year-old.

None of us mentions George's Ghost or George and Vi. We have no evidence yet so it would not be appropriate to do so.

When we meet up with Monaie's dad we ask him how he is. His response is

"I am fine but the Strattons have said that I stole the plane from them after we pretended to buy it from them and then we locked them in the cowshed after setting fire to their house. They believe we would have killed them in the fire. The police seem to have swallowed their version of events. The police have told me today that the Strattons want me prosecuted and the police have told me they also wish to prosecute me for Arson on top of Theft of a Light Aircraft and False Imprisonment of children. The police are awaiting the Fire Officer's report then they will almost definitely arrest me again."

"Before you ask, sis, Arson means deliberately setting fire to a place and is a crime, and False Imprisonment is holding children like us against their will, and is also a crime."

"But it wasn't **against** our will," I say with emotion nearly breaking my voice.

"I know that and you know that, sis, but that is what the Strattons have led the police to believe," Pete replies.

I say, "Pete, why is it that people can be so mean?"

Rob, who has until then kept still, now observes,

"What about the bags of money in the plane and the other bags? If we can get our hands on some of these while Monaie's dad is out on bail, we can get the police to believe our version of events."

This seems a great idea to us but others, inside the fire damaged cowshed, also have ideas of their own about collecting the money bags.

We need to act fast, I think.

"Well it's time to pay the river at the foot of Sloping Meadow another visit," Pete says.

"So soon?" jokes Rob and we all laugh.

"Just in case you have forgotten how wet and cold the river is!" jokes Giselle.

Claire is wrapped up today having developed a cold from being in the river last night.

Claire is not, unsurprisingly, amused, and sneezes just to prove it.

I stand next to Monaie and declare

"We must stand together now and help Monaie's dad obtain proof that the Strattons are up to no good then let the police have the proof so they can prosecute the right people instead of us."

"Yes," announces Monaie, eager to say anything, and once again we all laugh out loud but cannot fully explain to her as to why we are entertained by her remarks. She smiles as always and we each stroke her long hair with its ringlets as we pass her before her dad picks her up to carry her.

Outside, the skies are brighter now and looking north we can see traces of cerulean blue skies making their way over the open horizon above Sloping Meadow. It could well become a good day. The promise of a good day is certainly in the air.

Sloping Meadow itself looks inviting to us in spite of our late-night ordeal, so we march confidently on towards our destiny, hoping against hope, that we will meet our target and obtain the proof we need in order to help Monaie's dad, our brave pilot.

Just to keep the police less suspicious we all agree that only Giselle, Claire, Rob and Pete and, of course, I should go to try to retrieve some of the items from the plane currently sitting in the river. We feel it might be best if Monaie and her dad stay in their home just in case the police are watching them.

Monaie's dad agrees and takes Monaie up on his shoulders and leads them towards his own home.

It is now about ten a.m. and I can feel warm April sun on my back as we make our way towards the river.

Giselle, ever the enigmatic one, suddenly produces a carrot and offers it to the donkey which we meet on the edge of the meadow – the edge nearer to George's house.

After stroking the donkey who, by the way, is so soft to touch, possibly after all the heavy rain of last night helping to make him cleaner, we then become a little disorientated.

"Rob, I'll be honest, I am not brilliant with remembering the way anywhere," Pete informs Rob. Just then I can see about six wild Canadian Geese in the sky, flying in a "V" shape heading our way.

"They have to be heading for the river, Pete," I say.

"Oh, and what if they are heading away from the river?" Pete asks.

"I bet you they are heading towards the river," I say. "At this time of day, having slept the night in the woods for protection, they now need to eat on the river."

Pete's response is, "And I suppose you wish to be an ornithologist when you are older?"

"If you mean an expert on birds, no. I want to play football for England Women's Team!"

It was not long before the prospective England Player was proved correct.

After only about fifteen minutes, with the increased presence of mosquitoes adding to evidence of being nearer the water, we reached the river.

Rob's blond hair was flowing in the wind and he was whistling to his heart's content but, unknown to him, there was a low branch that he just got wacked by FULL IN HIS FACE.

THWACK!

We all laugh, much to his annoyance.

Suddenly, we spot a policeman standing looking bored, right by the place where, last night, the plane had slid noisily into the cold water.

We should have known that the plane would have been guarded by the police, as possible evidence of crime.

Perhaps it will show them our finger prints and confirm what the Strattons had told them. Who knows?

We all knew that it was almost impossible to get the policeman to leave his post unless we could come up with something.

The fact that he looked bored was in our favour.

It was Giselle who suddenly said to the policeman, "We just passed a hole in the ground, just back there, where we believe someone has dug something up from."

"And there is no chance it was a fox, neither," I added to help the bored policeman find some sort of interest.

"And there is no chance that it was a badger, neither," continued Giselle, looking as sweet and as innocent as she could. She raised her eyes and put her head to one side when speaking, just to heighten interest.

Rob then said, as quietly as he could to capture the man's full attention, "Well you hear all sorts don't you and, sometimes, the smallest things can lead to bigger things and before you know it someone is promoted at work just for coming up with something special – that's what I heard, in any case, and, what's more, that is what I believe."

"Well, I suppose I could just have a very quick look. Where did you say?"

"Just about ten minutes down the path back there," Claire said, pointing.

"You can't go anywhere near the plane, do you hear me now?"

"Of course we won't Officer," Rob confirmed.

The Officer made his way – fortunately he was quite heavily built – possibly why he had been tasked with just standing around looking after the plane, so he did not move fast.

It was Pete who volunteered to go into the water but Claire would have none of it.

"I am the best swimmer here and I should volunteer. In any event, I already have a cold so there's no danger of me getting another one is there?"

"Very well but remember all we need is one bag, or two at the very most."

Pete was right. If we could just get one or two of those bags up from the plane, it would be enough for us to get Monaie's dad out of the predicament that he found himself in and would help clear his good name.

Claire took her jeans off, after the boys had promised not to look at her, took a long hard breath in and plunged into the cold dark water. Without her jeans, she knew that she could swim faster.

She really had no idea just how cold that water would be but she valiantly swam down to the wreck of the plane.

"Cannot open the door yet!" she cried unhappily on surfacing. She stood dripping wet on the bank of the river shivering.

We now needed her so much to be successful.

I say to her, "Do your best but do it quickly before the policeman returns."

Claire bravely dives in again from the river bank this time and was gone. All I could see was great ripples of water and reflections of sunlight on the top of that water, but no Claire.

"She's been too long," I cry out after some time passes.

Claire surfaces with not one but two white bags. The boys grab her hands then the bags.

She is patted on the back by all of us and then, with great difficulty manages to put her jeans back on without the boys looking.

We are gone before you could say Pokémon.

We have no idea whether or not the policeman manages to find the hole that the Strattons had dug the bags out of and neither do we really care. We have done what we came to.

Job done.

With great luck Giselle spots the Strattons walking calmly towards us and we find it necessary to hide behind a clump of trees that still contain berries. After what seems like ages they pass us and we notice then that one of them has a heavy stick in his hands. We are able to get up and, with stiff legs from crouching down, make our way back to Monaie's house.

We knock hard on the door and tell Monaie's dad everything.

His decision is that, for now, we do nothing and just hope that they are spotted by the policeman. Having been sent to look for the hole in the ground it was unlikely the Strattons would be spotted by him for a while, but who knows?

We thank our lucky stars for spotting the Strattons before they came across us but we are also mindful of just how vulnerable all of us are now with them in the vicinity and looking for their bags of money.

With that thought Monaie's dad opens one white bag and we immediately see wads of banknotes in it. A lot of money.

When he then opens the other bag it contains credit cards and cheque books belonging to various persons. Stolen items!

"They are definitely up to no good," Pete says and we have to agree with him on this.

"Problem is," he continues, "just how to get this evidence to the police with the Strattons in Sloping Meadow and keen to stop us."

Chapter 17
Riding on a Donkey

The plan is for Giselle to ride the donkey. After all she has a rapport with it, having fed it a carrot only a short while ago. Under the donkey's belly will be hidden the two bags. They will be tied very carefully and will not show. The bags will be covered with cloth the same colour as the donkey – a purple grey.

April showers arrive unexpectedly. *Drip! Drip! Drip!*

We have no proper cover for this weather but who cares. We have to ensure that our plan works so we can help Monaie's dad. We suspect that the Strattons could be in the area but we are unsure.

Rob whistles but we are unsure if this is nervous or confident whistling.

"You would have to be psychic to know that we are carrying anything under the belly of that donkey," Monaie's dad says.

As usual, I ask what 'psychic' means and he replies "having special powers beyond the five senses we all have."

We have placed the two bags under the donkey and we are now ready to make the journey from Sloping Meadow to the police station in Kershalton.

We are determined in our quest and we will not take lightly to any interference.

The meadow lands leading up the main pathways are now water-logged and muddy but we keep going. Sloping Meadow looks majestic in the April showers. If anything, the colours of the meadow look sharper in the clean rain. Today the colours are greens, greys and the deepest of clay browns at once reflecting and absorbing the light, what little light there is, from the skies.

The sky is a burnt umber and shows us no cloud. The donkey is taking it all in its stride.

"What is the donkey's name?" I ask.

"Lucy, his name is Benjamin," cheerfully responds Monaie, sounding grown up.

"Ah! What a cool name," I observe.

"Sure is", adds Monaie's dad, "named after one of my best friends lost at sea when I was younger. Like his namesake the donkey is tough and hardy."

We all looked at Benjamin now in a different way, remembering that he had braved the storm the night before and had shown no fear.

Walking with an air of strength and grace we all thought Giselle looked very impressive, astride the donkey. For her first ever time on a donkey she was doing well. We all followed the donkey.

Benjamin occasionally even managed to eat the odd flowering shrub or two and Monaie's dad told us that they continuously eat the odd shrub or herb in order to medicate themselves when they are ill or are lacking in nutrients or minerals.

Monaie's dad informed us, "Did you youngsters realise that even Aspirin comes from the bark of a tree?"

No, we did not.

The April shower dripped its last drip and halted.

The sky instantly cheered up and now displayed yellow ochre and cerulean blue. I felt less unhappy about my parents blaming Monaie's dad and felt happier that finally we may be in a position to help him with the two bags proving the Stratton's criminal intent.

"Well, hello strangers," hissed a voice from the recent past. "What have we here, Jake?"

It was the shorter of the Strattons. He glared at me with weasel eyes. I realised, now that he was only inches from my face, that he not only smelt strongly of cigarettes but he also had no teeth in the bottom of his jaw.

He looked trouble and sure enough he matched his looks.

"He means 'Hello, Friends', of course, and thanks you all from his heart for trying to roast us like pigs on Stratton Farm. That's what he means," the taller of the Strattons said, through clenched and rotten teeth. He has not shaved for days.

Pete took one quick photo of him and you know what, he is so self-absorbed, I don't think that he even noticed. Certainly, he looked menacing and certainly he made us feel threatened. Here is Pete's photo so you can see why we did not like him.

Quickly we notice he is carrying what looks like a long handmade walking stick with a gnarled end to it that no doubt he would not hesitate to use on us.

"Now steady on you two. You know the police are about. You also know that we had no choice but to steal your plane and try to escape," Monaie's dad tells them.

"Keep quiet you," replied both men at once.

Just then they both zoom their eyes onto the lower parts of Claire's jeans.

"And just how did we manage to get our jeans so wet?" the taller one demands to know shaking the stick in one hand.

"It has been raining, you know," Rob responds calmly, trying to help Claire.

"Then how come the rest of you are much drier than she is?" the shorter of the two Strattons declares.

"Must have been in the river," he concludes. "Must have for sure, must have. Search them all. Every one of them!"

Both the Strattons move in and begin searching our bodies and clothes for any sign of their stolen bags.

They find nothing.

The taller Stratton, James, moves the stick menacingly around him then says, "Try the girl, Jake."

Jake, the shorter one, grabs her hair, pulling her off the donkey and searches her

"Nope. Nothing! Not a thing!"

"See you in Court, Grandad," the taller one says to Monaie's dad.

"Yeah, see you in Court, Grandad!" the shorter one echoes.

Both the Strattons seem happy when the illegal search of our bodies reveals nothing.

They both carry on towards the river but before they leave us they taunt Monaie's dad

"Can't prove anything, can you?"

Once again, Monaie's dad exercises his right to remain silent.

Claire cannot exercise her right to be silent as she is crying after being pulled off the donkey.

Chapter 18
Monaie's Dad Is Charged

Sure enough, Monaie's dad is charged with Taking and Driving away a Light Aircraft, False Imprisonment of Children and Arson.

In the Magistrates' Court, he pleads 'Not Guilty' to all three charges.

Due to an exceptional set of circumstances, largely due to a man changing his plea from Not Guilty to Guilty, Kershalton Crown Court will now hear the case today at two p.m. in an adjoining building.

Rob says, "We have to interrupt the case at the right time and bring in the evidence."

"Yes," Pete agrees. "But how do we do this?"

"Only an adult will be allowed in. We are doomed before we start. We have to trust the same policeman at the river today to realise that we are honest kids and need help."

Giselle is correct.

"Well the same policeman is on duty now in the Court Office. Look!" Pete shouts.

And so he is.

"I will talk to him and explain but let the trial begin first," I say.

Yes, poor old Monaie's dad has to face a trial.

The Judge in the Crown Court is wearing a smart white shirt and tie and looks, if anything, friendly.

We watch him arrive and enter his chambers. We are seated outside the courtroom.

Monaie's dad is placed in what they call the dock – basically this is the place where the accused person stands. He is still hand-cuffed.

The Judge enters the courtroom from his private room's door and the usher says clearly,

"Be upstanding for His Honour Judge Soames."

Everyone stands up, except for Monaie's dad, who is already standing.

The Judge briefly explains that in the Crown Court to be found guilty the jury of twelve men and women have to believe 'beyond reasonable doubt' that Monaie's dad is guilty.

If there is any doubt in their minds, they have to make a finding of Not Guilty in which case he will be a free man. Monaie's dad can see both the Strattons in the courtroom glaring at him with hatred.

They still want their money back but intend getting it tonight from the plane in the water.

Their spies have already told them the police will be lifting the plane out of the river tomorrow so they only have tonight to get their hands on their money bags and the other bags before the police do.

The Strattons, using their many associates, have made plans already to get their money back.

The prosecuting solicitor, acting for the Crown, outlines the charges and goes into great detail about it all.

The defending solicitor – this is the one acting for Monaie's dad – tries to outline what Monaie's dad's case is so the jury can decide whether he is guilty or not. Basically, Monaie's dad's defence is that he had no choice but to take the plane and save the kids as the two Stratton Brothers would have left them all in the cowshed tied up. They may have never been found alive.

The prosecuting solicitor then calls a witness, the Fire Chief, and immediately things are not looking good.

On oath, the Fire Chief lets the Court know that the evidence is clear that someone, probably Monaie's dad, deliberately set fire to the curtains of the Strattons' home – a thing that the Strattons would never do.

Monaie's dad maintains that this was done as a distraction so he could not only steal the plane but also take the kids with him.

When he is asked to give his version of what happened that night, Monaie's dad says that they were following two men who had dug up bags from the ground in Sloping Meadow that was his land. The chase led them to the Strattons and to Stratton Farm.

When the Strattons answered the door, and shone a light in their own back garden he had seen the Mercedes car that the two other men had used, so he knew there was a link between the Strattons and the two men who were seen digging up money.

After he had taken the plane which he readily admits to and it crash landed into the river the bags are still there in the river. If the police would care to search the plane he is sure his version can be corroborated. The Judge leans forward and directs that the jury must be made aware that, to date, there is no evidence that the sunken plane contains anything.

For now, they must consider the matter before them as a clean case of theft of a Light Aeroplane belonging to the Strattons. Additionally, the Jury must view the fire as deliberately set by the defendant to act as a distraction so he could more easily steal the plane.

Monaie's dad then admits that, "One of my party did set fire to the curtains, and the reason was so we could get the Strattons out of the cowshed where we were tied up and so we could steal the plane."

The Judge, looking as triumphant with all the strength and might of the Law of England behind him, turns to the jury and delivers the following, "Let the jury note that we are now witnessing an admission of guilt on the defendant's behalf and we must find him guilty of Theft of the Aeroplane and Arson. Two down – one to go."

It is true enough that if the judge can deal with this case swiftly he will be able to go straight to the golf course and play a round of golf.

However, just then, at the back of the Court appears the policeman from the river holding me by the hand.

"May I please approach the Court?" the policeman asks graciously, bowing to the Court. People bow when entering the Court because they are really bowing to what stands behind the Court, which is the Crown.

"Certainly, you may," the Judge directs.

"And who do we have the honour of addressing with you?"

"I am Lucy and I am a friend of Monaie and her dad." I say with force.

"The policeman has what you need," I continue.

"And what do think it is that I need?" the Judge demands to know.

"It is not what you need," I say, "but what the Court needs to have".

"And what is that young lady?" asks the Judge.

"Evidence," I respond.

The Judge laughs and says "You have interrupted my Court to lecture me on the Law of England and Wales."

"No, sir," I carry on. "I am here to help my friend's dad by bringing these two bags that Claire swam down deep to retrieve from the cold water."

"Here they are, your Honour," states the policeman, handing the two white bags to the Court Steward.

The Judge instructs the usher to open them in front of the jury and two men immediately leave their seats to run out of the Court but the policeman grabs one by the arm and trips the other up.

In no time at all the Court clearly sees who are the guilty men and who the innocent.

The Judge, after some time looking carefully at the contents, calls for a break in proceedings then at three p.m. reconvenes the Court.

"Well, Monaie's dad, as the lovely Lucy has referred to you before the break, it is clear that the Crown owes you a huge apology. Please accept this Court's apologies for your arrest and trial today."

The Judge looks at me and says, "It is my pleasure to direct the jury to find you, Frank Darby, not guilty of all charges. This means that you are a free man!"

Outside the courtroom I can hear Rob, Pete, Claire and Giselle cheer.

The social worker allows Monaie to run straight up to her dad and hug him and kiss him forty times with joy.

Jake Stratton and James Stratton are both immediately arrested for many counts of criminal behaviour and will face trial soon. They are held in custody and our guess is that they will remain in custody for many years to come.

We all feel good but are very tired so we make our way back home at four p.m. and when I walk in to my house mum asks me, "Did you do anything?"

"Not much," I reply.

How cool is my response to her?

Chapter 19
Back Now to the Matter of George

Tuesday morning and the whole of Kershalton Village is discussing the Strattons and how wicked their behaviour has been, not only towards Monaie's dad but also to those they have stolen money and credit cards from.

So, while most of the village and neighbouring towns and villages are carefully checking their credit card statements and cheque books and cash balances, we creep out of our houses and head towards Monaie's house with full permission to use the side gate in Sloping Meadow and cross into George's garden unseen by anyone.

Monaie is with her dad and I am now walking with Rob, Claire, Giselle and my brother Pete. We are still looking for answers for poor old George who lost his finger, then his life.

We still care about why he died and who was responsible for his death. We still care about where his body is.

We now feel that we are stronger by what we have achieved for Monaie's dad and head off towards the gate.

By the gate I stop, because just as we approach, I notice a very large common toad crawling slowly away from us.

"Not you again with the animals," Pete shouts in my face pretending to be angry.

"They are not animals but are amphibians," I reply.

"Of course," he says "I know that, I even know their Latin name: Bufo Bufo."

We all pause momentary to admire yet another of Mother Nature's wonderful creatures.

I am at my best when confronted head on by nature and its many splendid sights and sounds.

The wet grasses of Sloping Meadow make us long for summer and its dryness as we leave it for the gate we all know now as Monaie's Gate.

The day looks, in spite of its dampness, perfect.

I am not perfect myself. I have weaknesses. I think I criticise other friends too much. Mum says if I am aware of this fault it will enable me to improve on it.

I am not wholly wrapped up in myself sometimes. Mum says that if I am unhappy about any aspect about myself it can change, for example, if I am unhappy about my height I am still growing and can get taller. If my Maths is not good I can do extra lessons and improve.

Mum drums it into me to make the most of what I have come into the world with. I am me and if that means having short or long legs, being pretty or not so pretty, being sometimes sad and sometimes feeling not as good as others then I have to challenge those feelings and ask why is it I think I am not as good as others. Now it might be that I will never be good enough to play Women's Football for England but I can always play football at some level that suits my footballing skills.

There is nothing wrong in having dreams but, let's be straight about it, if you can't play the violin you will never make the London Symphony Orchestra as their number one violinist, so there's no point in being unrealistic about your dreams. Stay real.

We have all come into the world to experience things and to hopefully develop so we may as well make the most of it and do our best to stay healthy and not to do anything to harm any creature or any person. That's what I believe and mum agrees with me. Mum says that we all have our time in our lives when we can shine – when it is just our time. With my thoughts soaring high like the goldfinches do, I trip up some clump of bracken and land flat on my face!

Rob says, "Lucy, enjoy your trip."

Giselle, Claire, and my brother all laugh.

Giselle helps me up and we talk about life. "Do you ever feel that you have a small voice in your head that tells you, before you even ask it, that you will not be able to do something well when you plan to do something?" I ask Claire.

She replies, "What I think is that we all have this negative side to us that tries to put us down or put us off doing something new or exciting. I think it is called being human."

"Well, how do you deal with it?"

"I just tell it to go away and do whatever it is that I want to do. I suppose I take no notice of it."

"So it's not just me then that hears this voice."

"No," Giselle says, brushing her hair out of her face, "it's all of us."

"I will definitely use your tactic and tell it to go away from now on. Thank you."

"I wish someone had told me this when I was younger though because it took me ages to pluck up the courage to tell it to go away."

"And when you did?" I asked.

"And when I did, it went away, Lucy, it went far away."

Pete interrupts Rob's whistling to announce, "We are now coming near to where we found George's finger. Quiet please, everyone, especially no whistling until we know what we are doing next."

"Can we please have a discussion about what that is?" asks Giselle.

"About what what is?" enquires Pete, slightly annoyed in having his leadership questioned.

"About what we are doing next," Giselle states calmly.

"Look, Pete, no one is challenging your authority to have the final say but we need to discuss what we believe to be the best way forward." I say matter-of-factly.

"Okay, sis, I see what you are saying. Does anyone here wish to suggest what we do? There are a few options. While the entire village is preoccupied with their cash we could try a couple of things."

"Like what?" Giselle responds.

"Like all trying to get into George's house and see what is going on and if we can obtain any evidence of what may have happened to him."

"This appeals to me," Claire states, happy to please Pete.

"Can I suggest we look carefully around the garden again, maybe for a burial site," Giselle says.

"Are you saying that he may have been buried by Vi in his own garden?" Pete says.

It is Rob who replies

"Why ever not? It's been done before, you know."

Pete sits down and asks for a show of hands.

Giselle, Rob, and Claire vote to look around and Pete and I to look inside the house.

Both options are viable.

Pete then says, "Looks like we are going to be searching the garden around the house but be careful. We do not want to be seen or caught by anyone."

We all nod our agreement.

"We will split up. Lucy and I will look at the left side and Claire Rob and Giselle the right."

Pete and I walk towards the back of the house and it is not long before we come across what looks like a long grave riddled with earthworms.

I shudder and say, "Well, Pete, it is long enough and wide enough for a grave."

We both prod it and poke it gingerly, sending the worms back under the earth, and soon Pete declares, "Too narrow for a grave. Far too narrow and it is full of compost so any flowers can grow better. Must therefore be a flower bed."

We both laugh and carry on looking.

Giselle, Claire and Rob have now come across what looks like a cellar window well below the windows which we assume must lead down to a cellar.

"An old coal cellar?" Claire suggests.

"Or a place to keep and hide a body?" suggests Giselle.

"A fingerless body!" Rob concludes.

"You sure know how to make a girl frightened!" I shout at him, as by now, Pete and I have caught up with them.

"You scared me!" Rob admits.

"Well, you must have scared Claire and Giselle," I say.

"Rob, stop trying to scare us!" Claire says.

"Sorry," Rob says and he means it.

We decide to try to open the grated iron window cover that sits on top of the casement window that leads down to the cellar room and are surprised to find that it opens if we all pull hard on the railings covering it.

We push it sideways and Pete climbs down.

"Be careful," I say in a sisterly way.

"You're all coming down too," Pete says and we begin to descend into the dank cellar after we have managed to open the only window. Pete crosses the small cellar room and then we spot it.

A body lies under what appears to be a mound of curtains.

Our hearts miss a beat and our stomachs turn to jelly.

Pete then carefully pulls the curtains off the corpse, revealing a bronze statue of a Roman Soldier, green in parts due to a chemical change caused by the weather.

We gasp at the shock of seeing it and feel relief that it is not a real body.

"Thank God it's just a statue!" Rob says.

"Yes. And now can we go?" Claire says.

"We need to see if this door here opens." Pete says.

When he opens the door, it opens with a great CREAKING SOUND!

The door opens and Vi walks in, putting the light on.

"Thought I heard some noise. Thought it was rats or something. But it is actually children. You lot from opposite. Are you not the kids from across the way?"

"Yes we are," Pete says, too shocked to think of a reason why we were even there in her cellar room.

"Vi, we are sorry to be trespassing on your property but we have lost Billy the cat!" Giselle says.

"Well indeed, I guess you can't help looking for a cat you love, can you?"

"No," Rob says.

"We did not think anyone was in and Giselle saw it come down this cellar bit... or thought she had," Claire says.

"Okay. Children, the first thing you should have done is knocked on my door and asked permission to search the garden and house for your cat."

"I know that now. We are sorry. Please accept our apologies and we can climb out of here and go home." Pete was right we needed to get away, as far away from her as we could.

"I can tell you Billy the cat is not inside my house but you can search the gardens if you wish. Also try the man next door, who owns Sloping Meadow."

"Sure will, Vi," I say quickly.

We began climbing out of the cellar and out of the casement window as fast as we could, wondering constantly if she was going to murder us next.

The quicker we tried to leave her, however, the slower it seemed to happen. We all felt a bit uneasy about blaming Vi when we were not quite sure of what, if anything, she had done to George.

Mum says if you wish to blame anyone for doing something wrong then you must have proof. Currently we have nothing.

We need to find something that links her to George's death or his death to her, if that makes sense.

It makes sense to me anyhow.

Chapter 20
The Ghost Pays Vi a Visit

Finally, the last to leave the damp cellar is Pete, who rather gallantly decides to stay the longest with the alleged murderer.

Pete says, "I think we should go to the lounge windows, just to see what Vi does next."

We make our way around to the lounge windows from where earlier, on being held by Rob, my superhero, I previously had seen the lovely copy of a Degas painting.

We look in.

This time I am being held by my brother, Pete. *Not as strong as Rob*, I think, but I would not dare tell him. You know what boys are like? They like to think of themselves as the strongest and the bravest.

We are now in for a shock because we now see George's ghost appear suddenly and this time he suddenly rises from the floor.

Vi shouts something at him then raises her hands in the air and rushes out of the room. She looks terrified and guilty all at once.

Rob's blond hair stands on end. We can never ever get used to ghosts, no matter how hard we try.

"Well that confirms her guilt!" Rob says.

"Could do but we still have no proof she killed him," I say, having learned today that evidence is everything.

Mum used to say that we learn things when we are ready to learn them.

There is probably a correct natural time in which to learn things and our time is not yet.

We have to keep looking for our evidence. "I know, if we tell Monaie's dad what we know, we could ask him to accompany us and we could then confront Vi with him on our side and watch how she plays it all." Pete says.

"I like this idea," Claire says and Giselle agrees.

"After all," I say, "we helped Monaie's dad and now we need help ourselves. One good turn deserves another."

Everyone nods their agreement so we begin to make our way back towards Monaie's house.

I notice snowdrops out – their brightness makes the grasses – yellow and green, seem even more vibrant.

Somehow we all feel we may be heading in the right direction by involving our trusted Pilot, Monaie's dad.

We cross over through Monaie's gate and past Benjamin who greets us with a deep braying noise sounding just like a cow. We pass and, as we do, Giselle hugs him but he nonchalantly carries on eating the grasses that comprise his main diet now that spring has arrived. It is good to see him looking healthy and happy and it is good to cross into Sloping Meadow again. There is something about Sloping Meadow that I have come to love. I think *in my dreams I must visit this place.*

This place holds rich memories for all – not all good ones – but all treasured for the experiences that we as friends have shared.

Monaie runs towards us in her riding gear so *she must have been having riding lessons* I think.

"Oh, no, not riding lessons. Dad bought me this to try on today. I love it and the riding hat," she informs me when asked.

"Well," Pete declares, "You certainly look the part."

"Thank you, Pete," Monaie says. "My lessons with dad start next week."

"Right. Well good luck with them. Is dad in so we can ask him something?" Pete enquires.

"He's in," Monaie says.

We all are invited in, first by Monaie, then by her dad.

"How are we all today?"

"We are well, sir," replies Rob for all of us.

Once comfortably seated we do our best, without interrupting each other too much, to explain about George, George's finger and George's death, even remembering the December promise of seeing the newts in April. We then explain about George's shed, George's Ghost and how we have seen the Ghost in the shed fire and in the house with Vi his wife, who we have reason to believe has killed him and cut him up. Oh, and we even remember to tell him about the Ghostly Violin Player – when Vi most certainly cannot play the violin, proving it had to be George's ghost.

We satisfy Monaie's dad on every count that George is dead and has visited his widow, Vi.

Except for one.

HOW DID WE LEARN OF GEORGE'S DEATH?

"My brother told me just as though he were reading the news, in front of my friends and in my home," I declare.

Rob confirms this, as do Claire and Giselle.

"This is true," they say together.

Pete then says, "This is indeed the truth."

Monaie's dad then says, "Forgive me for asking but how did you find this out?"

Pete say, "I heard Vi say, rather shout it, on the phone as I passed the house. That's how I know for sure that he has died."

"Oh dear!" Monaie's dad says respectfully, "May God bless his soul!"

We explain rapidly that we need him now. We need him to give up his time and come with Monaie to help us confront Vi, who, we believe knows where his fingerless body lies. We need to ask her outright.

"WHERE IS GEORGE'S BODY AND WHAT HAVE YOU DONE TO HIM?"

Monaie's dad readily agrees to come but just in case of trouble he will bring his old trusty walking stick that was given to him by his dad. The stick has a top that can be unscrewed to pour Brandy in.

We agree to this and we begin to consider what lies ahead.

Giselle offers, "I don't mind asking her the most salient questions."

Pete explains to me that, by 'salient', she means the most pressing questions and the ones that need answers.

"Thanks, Pete," I reply.

"What makes me think that today is going to be a difficult day for Vi?"

"And for us," Giselle adds.

Monaie's dad offers us toast which we eat, especially Rob, then we all leave together for George's old home.

For better or worse we make our way around to poor George's home. Giselle knocks on the door confidently, starting as she means to continue.

Chapter 21
Explanations and Conclusions

Vi comes to the door immediately looking annoyed.

"Not you children again!" she shouts.

Monaie's dad shows himself and says to her firmly, "Now there's no need to shout."

This takes her aback and she then says, "How can I assist you all on this occasion?"

Giselle asks her, "We need your permission please to come in. Please may we come in?"

Vi is reluctant and says "If you could all come back say in an hour this would suit me better."

We all think that this is just what she needs: another hour, in which to escape the house where she has murdered her husband George.

"No way!" Giselle says. "We have a few salient questions to ask you and need to talk to you now."

"If you insist," she concedes.

"Yes we do insist," Monaie's dad says.

"Come in but I must insist that you get to the point very quickly as I am very busy."

Giselle waits until we are all comfortably seated before she addresses her questions to Vi.

"We found George's finger, his bloody finger, in the long grass near the pond. We have reason to believe that you have had something to do with this. We have reason to believe that we have seen his fingerless ghost appearing to us on more than one occasion, desperately trying to contact us…"

She stops speaking because at that moment in time George's ghost appears suddenly in the room and says loud and clear

"I have searched high and low for my finger; where was it?"

All of us say "**OH MY GOD GEORGE'S GHOST!**"

Monaie's dad nearly faints and holds his chest.

Giselle is the only one who then finds her voice to say

"You have been appearing because you needed to find your finger before you could properly pass into the next world?"

"Eh! No! I was looking for my finger to take it to Accident & Emergency, at St Helier Hospital, to have it maybe sewn back on but sadly I could not find it to place it in ice so it could be saved and stitched back on."

I say "You mean you are not a ghost anymore?"

"I never was, nor ever have been, a ghost, not now not ever, NEVER!"

"My dad saw a ghost once on a ship!" Monaie whispers.

We all laugh loud and long and we continue to laugh for many minutes to come.

"So Vi never chopped you up and couldn't find your finger after cutting it off?" Rob asks.

"No," George says, "I was cutting logs with my Scorpion Electric Saw and cut my index finger clean off by accident!"

"What about the ghostly violin?" Rob continues.

"When we both got back from the hospital I wanted to see if I could still use my violin bow to play my violin, which I could. It will always be possible."

Claire then says, "Well what about the fact that we saw you burning in the shed fire. It was well hot and yet you just stood there looking at us."

"I went down to the shed because I saw a light on there – it was probably your phone light or a candle. When I got to the shed I saw a fire had started with a low candle spilling onto the table. I did what I could to move the petrol can for the mower for fear of an explosion."

"But," I say, "You looked right at us like a ghost would."

"I did not have my glasses on. I would not have seen you or anyone at that time without my glasses."

Pete who had been quiet had two more points to make: "Firstly, what about when the American Pit Bull was chasing our boat across the river and it stopped, yelped, then turned back when it saw a ghost?"

"The reason it responded like that was simple. I had occasion to whip it with a stick as it attacked me about four days ago and it remembered the pain I inflicted. Oh by the way, I had no choice as it would have tried to kill me. If I had not whipped it with a strong stick I would have incurred terrible injuries. The dog is, I believe, ill and will attack anyone. I have reported that dog to the police but they called round to my house the other day to tell me they could not find it."

Pete looks at the floor and manages to say "Oh".

"And your second point is?" demands George.

"What about when at the riverside you left no footprints?"

"It was heavy rain. Footprints would not be seen after heavy rain."

Pete stared at the ghost of George and then in desperation said,

"What about the phone call I overheard? Vi had said 'George died!'"

"You, my boy, should not listen to phone calls," Vi shrieked with laughter. "I was explaining to my friend that I would be late for our game of cards because I was taking George to the hospital as he had cut off a finger and nearly died. When this friend asked me 'George nearly did what?' I had shouted '**DIED**'."

"So you guys thought I was dead," George said seeing the funny side of the whole matter.

"**OH MY GOD!**" we all said.

Monaie then said, "I am Monaie. What was it like George?"

George replied "What was what like, Monaie?"

"What was it like being dead?" she said and again we laughed and could not explain it to her why we had laughed so much and for so long.

Both George and Vi then told us all that we were always going to be welcome to come and call on them, and look at the pond whenever we wanted, especially when we had given them both such a good laugh.

On the way home, with Monaie's dad carrying Monaie, we skipped and laughed happy for George and for Vi.

Monaie's dad pointed out that it possibly happened for a reason otherwise those Stratton Brothers would have got away with all their crimes and many would have suffered financially.

When we reached Monaie's house we said goodbye to Monaie and to Benjamin the donkey and to Monaie's lovely dad. And, just for a little while, we hoped, we also said goodbye to Sloping Meadow – the loveliest place to be on Earth.

On our way home, we then decided to play one more game of RIDIQ and Pete, this time, for his most ridiculous statement said out loud, making us all laugh again: "**The Man Opposite has died.**"

We all agreed that this was the most ridiculous statement we had heard that day.

When I finally arrived at my home mum asked me

"Did you do anything?"

"Not much," I replied.

How cool am I?

THE END OF THE FIRST BOOK OF THE SLOPING MEADOW TRILOGY